Praise for Susan Fox:

About THE MARRIAGE BARGAIN

"The Marriage Bargain is a must read
with spellbinding characters..."
—*Romantic Times*

About TO CLAIM A WIFE

"Fans will relish Ms. Fox's fabulous characters
and emotionally intense plot."
—*Romantic Times*

About THE WIFE HE CHOSE

"Susan Fox offers a touching read that captures
the dynamics of a developing relationship."
—*Romantic Times*

Susan Fox lives with her youngest son, Patrick, in Des Moines, Iowa, U.S.A. A lifelong fan of Westerns and cowboys, she tends to think of romantic heroes in terms of Stetsons and boots! In what spare time she has, Susan is an unabashed couch potato and movie fan. She particularly enjoys romantic movies, and also reads a variety of romance novels—with guaranteed happy endings—and plans to write many more of her own.

Susan Fox has a compelling writing style and loves to take her characters on an intense emotional journey! Share in the powerful feelings and dilemmas experienced by her hero and heroine in Susan's latest novel. The path to true love never runs smoothly, but the thrill of the chase will keep you hooked!

Books by Susan Fox

Don't miss any of our special offers. Write to us at the following address for information on our newest releases.

Harlequin Reader Service
U.S.: 3010 Walden Ave., P.O. Box 1325, Buffalo, NY 14269
Canadian: P.O. Box 609, Fort Erie, Ont. L2A 5X3

THE PRODIGAL WIFE
Susan Fox

TO HAVE AND TO HOLD

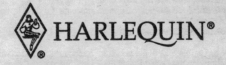

HARLEQUIN®

TORONTO • NEW YORK • LONDON
AMSTERDAM • PARIS • SYDNEY • HAMBURG
STOCKHOLM • ATHENS • TOKYO • MILAN • MADRID
PRAGUE • WARSAW • BUDAPEST • AUCKLAND

ISBN 0-373-03740-6

THE PRODIGAL WIFE

First North American Publication 2003.

CHAPTER ONE

GABE PATTON and Lainey Talbot had been married for almost five years, though they'd only been together in the same room twice since then. The first time was that ten minutes after a judge had pronounced them husband and wife as they'd signed the marriage certificate. She'd coldly walked out without a word to Gabe, leaving the beautiful rings he'd just put on her finger lying next to her signature.

The second time had been at her mother's funeral six months ago. She'd kept herself aloof, wordlessly listening to Gabe's formal expression of condolence before she'd stoically endured less than an hour breathing the same air as him while the memorial service droned on.

She'd walked away from him that time, too. Calmly and coldly, still frozen from the shock of her mother's death, but still quite coldly furious with him for what he and her late father had done to her.

Over the five years she'd spent away from Texas and Gabe Patton, she'd refused his every phone call, and sent back to him, unopened, every letter and gift he'd sent to her. Still self-righteous, she'd boldly marked on each envelope or package in red felt pen: Refused. Return To Sender.

She'd never acknowledged Gabe Patton as her legal husband in even a remote way, much less taken his name, though she'd been forced to file her income tax returns as married, filing single, and she'd had to instruct her lawyer to rebuff any attempt at contact, short of death or a divorce petition. She hadn't let herself think many good thoughts about Gabriel Patton; she'd certainly never spoken anything good about him these past years.

She'd almost managed to make herself forget the mad adolescent crush she'd had on him once when she was barely eighteen, and she'd staunchly tried to deny to herself the reasons she'd loved him to distraction back then. Sometimes she was even successful. She'd been glad she'd taken such incredible pains to protect her female pride, to keep a wary distance from Gabe Patton so he'd never suspect her feelings for him—particularly once she'd found out that the only reason he'd agreed to marry her had been to get control of Talbot Ranch.

Her sweet, agonizing crush had exploded into fiery hate when he'd done that, and she'd sworn to herself that she'd never show Gabriel Patton an ounce of welcome or approval as a husband. Never.

But she'd got it wrong, so very wrong.

Gabe Patton had never been the greedy opportunist she'd thought he was when he'd agreed to the marriage deal her father had secretly cooked up for his only child. A marriage deal she'd never suspected until after her father's sudden death when she'd heard the barbaric terms of his will.

In her mind, the father she'd idolized had apparently found a way to punish her for trying to stay neutral in his bitter divorce from her mother. John Talbot had never given any indication of disapproval toward her and had even seemed to agree with her decision when she'd left the ranch to live with her mother in Chicago. But when he'd given away control of her inheritance to the man he'd selected for her to marry, she'd taken it as a brutal revelation of some virulent, secret anger her father had harbored over the agonizing choice she'd made.

And because her much-loved and adored father had been just four days dead by the time she'd found it out, she hadn't been able to bring herself to be angry with him, only wounded and bewildered by what he'd done. Instead she'd taken out her rage over the shock of her father's death, and the injustice of his secret bargain, on Gabe. She'd spurned him and done spite to the marriage that had been forced on her.

Until her mother had died and she'd read the truth in the ream of papers and documents Sondra had hidden away from her and lied about. Everything

Lainey had done, every cold act, had been based on lies and pain and more lies. Because of what her mother had engineered, Lainey had not only dishonored her husband and her marriage, she'd also dishonored the memory of the loving father who'd tried to protect her from her mother's greed, then had suddenly died before he could explain his reasons.

Now the stench of dishonor was slowly poisoning her soul. For weeks she'd been traumatized by the truth, and every moment of those weeks, sharp guilt had eaten at her and sickening questions had pounded her heart.

Was there a way to make up these past five years to Gabriel Patton? Was there anything she could do to somehow atone for the things she'd done to him—and his pride—in a way that might at least mollify him and give him some sort of satisfaction? It was too much to expect that he could forgive her. She'd come to that heart-crushing conclusion when she'd read the truth and realized the magnitude of her hatefulness.

If he paid her back even a smidgen of what she'd done to him, it would be the much deserved and overdue justice that was owed to a wronged man.

He'd endured her venom for years without a hint of retaliation, so he deserved to hear her admit to his face what she should have known all along: that he was an honorable man of character who was far too good for her, not the come-from-nothing lowlife she'd believed he was.

As terrified as she was to see him again and endure whatever awful things he'd say to her now, it was only right that she take whatever he was willing to dish out and do it without complaint.

Every air mile between Chicago and Patton Ranch had been a small eternity, surpassed only by the endless miles she'd driven from San Antonio in a rented car. Her crisply ruffled white blouse and khaki slacks were not exactly sackcloth, but she fretted over the selection. Had styling her long, dark hair in a chic upsweep made her look too aloof and citified? Should she have worn jeans and a simple cotton blouse, or should she have dressed even more like a spoiled princess who deserved to be mocked and chastised?

As long as the trip had seemed to take, the main house appeared suddenly over the last shallow rise of ranch road. Lainey's heart surged into her throat and thumped fast and hard. She felt perspiration dot her face as another wave of guilt and terror washed painfully through her.

The large single-story adobe ranch house had a new addition on the east, and the gleaming rows of the new red tile roof gave the white-painted adobe below a pristine glow. The deep, shady veranda stretched along the entire front of the house, and each arch that curved over its outer edge was decorated with hanging pots of trailing flowers that favored deep blues and rich purples with touches of more red.

The luster of fresh red paint on the huge double front doors hinted that they could be either the gates of a threatening hell or the redemptive color of a joyous heaven. Lainey was well aware of which one she'd forfeited and which one she deserved.

Shame sent a hot flush to her face as she got out of the rental car, took out her handbag and leather briefcase, then made herself start up the front walk. The briefcase was heavy, perhaps because the papers and documents inside that vindicated Gabe were also an indictment of her stupidity.

The documents her mother had forged were also in the case, and she felt another twist of her insides at the thought that however evil it had been of her mother to perpetrate them on her, showing them to Gabe now would be as self-serving as it was disloyal to her mother.

Her feelings about her mother were still in turmoil. Was she being disloyal or was Sondra even worthy of loyalty after what she'd done?

But on the issue of selfishness, Lainey knew she was guilty. She still had the wild, impossible hope that when she showed the papers and forgeries to

Gabe, he would understand, have mercy on her, and forgive her for the way she'd treated him.

She didn't know what would happen after that. Probably divorce. There could be no reason that Gabe would want her after she'd been such a horror as a wife.

Then again, he might never see the papers. If he decided to pay her back in kind, he'd give her no opportunity to explain her actions. He'd probably throw her—and her briefcase of papers—out of his house and chase her off Patton Ranch. If that happened, she'd begin divorce proceedings next month. No sense being a millstone around his neck any longer.

Nausea began the slow, sickening climb into her chest as she reached the red doors and put out her free hand to push the doorbell. As if the housekeeper had seen her drive up and had been waiting for her to ring, the big red door on the right was pulled open.

Lainey didn't recognize the Hispanic woman, but bid her a quiet, "*Buenos dias, señora.* Lainey Talbot to see Señor Patton."

No doubt the woman would know her name whether she recognized Lainey or not. And sure enough, a faint light of suspicion and disapproval showed in the woman's dark eyes, though her reserved smile was polite.

"Buenos dias. Señor Gabe is out with the men today. Perhaps you could come back at evening."

"Is there any way I can go out wherever he is to speak to him?" Lainey asked hastily, suddenly worried that this might be her sole opportunity to see Gabe. She'd purposely not let him know ahead of time that she was coming. It was a sneaky thing to do, but she'd been afraid she'd never get near him otherwise.

Her only option then would be to get her lawyer to contact his lawyer. And again, Gabe had tried that periodically with her, but her instructions to her attorney had been another hateful rebuff.

To her surprise and relief, the woman seemed to make a decision about her, though it was clear she was hesitant about it.

"I can try to contact him for you."

Relief gave Lainey a fraction of hope. "That would be very kind. I can wait out here."

Lainey had added that last to somehow communicate to the woman that she understood the predicament her request had put her in. Gabriel Patton's employees were loyal to him, and it would be unfair to put a strain on that.

She'd also meant the offer to wait outside the house as a semi-public acknowledgment that she had no right to cross the threshold into Gabe's private domain. A wife like her didn't deserve that kind of access.

The woman nodded and stepped back, making a polite smile again before slowly closing the door.

The nausea climbed a bit higher, and Lainey turned miserably to stare at the land. It was so abominably hot, but then it was just past two p.m., and this was June in Texas. Her body had become too accustomed to her air-conditioned life in Chicago.

Nevertheless, the sight of pastureland between the house and the highway nearly two miles distant was a visual comfort. It was also the only comfort she'd felt in weeks now, and she began to feel faintly shocked that she could have walked away from ranch life and endured the cement-surrounded life of the city for so long.

Oh, God, if I could come back to this...

The door behind her opened again and she turned back, trying not to reveal the pitiful hope she had. The housekeeper's face showed little more than her polite smile and that same touch of wary disapproval.

"Señor Gabe is bringing horses to the pens now. He says you may meet him there or not, but he is too busy to come to you."

Lainey tried to find some encouragement in that. If Gabe was allowing her to come that close to him, surely it was a good sign, though it was apparently all he was willing to do. The only time she'd allowed him a chance to be anywhere in her vicinity had been six months ago at the funeral. Perhaps this was a turn-about-is-fair-play sort of thing. She'd only been barely civil to him that one time, so maybe this would be the only time he'd be barely civil to her.

"Thank you, *señora,*" she said, then turned to rush to her car and put her handbag and briefcase inside. She started around the big house to the buildings and corrals of the headquarters.

Her brain was so awhirl with thoughts of what to say during the long walk that she didn't realize until she'd passed the last of the buildings that her sandals were now gritty with dirt. The ground had been sun-baked and churned by so many hooves that the dirt was powdery.

As she stopped to scan the panorama of ranch land ahead, she saw the rising dust of a small herd of horses moving steadily in her direction and gave up on any thought of going back to the car for her boots. She took up a position next to the open gate of one of the larger pens, then shaded her eyes with her hands as she tried to pick Gabe out from the three men who were moving the horses along at a slow pace in the afternoon heat.

Her heart began to tremble with fear and excitement. Fear because she didn't know what Gabe would say or do; excitement because the sight of young horses being brought in, probably for training, was familiar. It had been ages since she'd been on a horse, and she was suddenly emotional over the sight. She'd missed so much!

Lainey searched the size and posture of the three men, but even from a distance, she could tell that none of them were Gabe. She lowered her hands a moment, then was compelled to look again, fretting. Had he changed his mind about seeing her?

After another long, futile look, she lowered her hands again. A movement in her peripheral vision drew her to glance that way briefly, and she felt the shock of what she saw go from her brain to her feet.

Gabe Patton sat astride a huge black gelding, and he was watching her with an iron calm that sent another shock pounding through her. The horse's neck and flank were damp, and his big hooves moved restively, as if he was eager to run.

Five years had only hardened Gabe Patton's rugged looks, and they carried a seasoned harshness that she'd never seen. He'd been wearing a suit at the service six months ago, but his face had not been harsh, merely somber. Today it was decidedly stony. And unreadable. Gabe had never been handsome, but he carried the look of a westerner who worked hard and somehow he'd achieved such a devastating male charisma that, after this, would make it impossible for her to ever be impressed with softer, more conventionally handsome men.

His big body also looked harder and stronger—he was as tall as a giant—adding to a larger-than-life presence that was more potent and compelling for her than ever before, even six months ago. But she'd been trying not to look at him much then, and she was now getting the full view of a man who showed not a flicker of the sympathy she'd read in his expression during the ten or so seconds she'd actually looked at him that day.

Gabe was in his element here in the outdoors, so his impact on her seemed unchecked and unrestrained. She wondered dazedly if perhaps he somehow toned himself down in more civilized, indoor places, and she made a fervent wish that he would do it now. Instead he seemed to become more intimidating by the moment.

Beneath the shade of his black Stetson his dark eyes glittered slowly over her from head to foot as if he was judging the confirmation of a horse he might buy—or cull. She saw the faint curl of weary mockery that indented one side of his hard mouth, then saw it suddenly vanish as his dark gaze slid up from her dirty sandals and feet to slam against hers.

Anger, suspicion and something flat and icy showed in his gaze before he loosened the reins a fraction and his huge horse minced toward her. The sight made her think of a knight in full armor on a black destrier who could charge forward at any second to enter a battle to the death. When he stopped his big horse beside her and she turned to look up at him, the width of his shoulders blocked the sun. The heat from his horse was scorching, but she stood her ground.

Gabe was still staring harshly down at her, and she was helpless to look away. Her brain felt the deep probe of his gaze like a rough touch. She got nothing more from the way he looked at her than the impression that he was searching for something of worth in a place where searching for worth might be a waste of time.

Suddenly terrified that he'd stare at her a few moments more then just ride away, she managed to say, "I'm sorry." The words croaked out of her dry throat, but he heard them.

"Sorry for what?" he said at last. "Sorry you had to come all this way, sorry you got your feet dirty?"

Now he would get his pound of flesh—that much was plain in the bitter way he said the words. But she'd come here to do some sort of penance and she hadn't truly expected anything but harshness, whatever her wild hopes had been. She tried to take this as calmly and patiently as he'd taken all her slights and mistreatments.

"C-can we go someplace to talk?" The tremor in her voice was impossible to thwart.

"No reason until you answer the question. Sorry for what?"

She suddenly couldn't bear the diamond glitter in his eyes and looked away. She'd craved this opportunity for weeks while she worked up her courage, but Gabe was so tough and skeptical of her that she wished she could simply vanish from his sight and slink away somewhere.

But if she let him chase her off now, she'd regret that, too, and she might never get another chance.

"I came here to…apologize." The dryness in her mouth and the surge of roiling emotions complicated it all. "To even grovel if that's…what it takes."

Now she made the monumental effort to look up at him again, to say this to his face as she'd meant to. "I've been awful to you. You were never what I thought you were, and I came here to tell you that. And to say that I'm profoundly sorry."

The diamond glitter in his eyes was suddenly banished by dark fire. "So now you want a divorce."

His conclusion sent a new shock through her and she reflexively gave a quick, "No," then caught herself and just as quickly added, "Yes. But you can't want to stay married to me."

The fire in his eyes didn't lower by so much as a

spark, so she rushed out with, "Isn't that what you want to do?"

He let her wait a few more breathless seconds before he leaned toward her. She had to fight not to take a step back. "You have no idea what I *want* to do."

To beat her, strangle her? The way he'd said the word *want* seemed menacing enough to suggest those things.

"Could we talk?"

Nothing eased in his face or in his eyes, but his voice lowered to a growl. "You've always taken the say-so about that."

She tried a small, conciliatory smile, but it felt more like a sick curve of lips. She was just so desperate to somehow win a chance to tell him everything she'd come here to say. "I'm sorry about that, too." Her heart was beating impossibly fast. "It's your turn now."

Not getting any clue that she'd said enough to satisfy him, she panicked and babbled out, "It's completely your turn now, Gabe, completely."

She couldn't bear the awful suspense and her breathless, "Could we?" came out without her being conscious of it until she heard herself say the words. She'd sounded like a pitiful child begging for something, and she cringed inwardly. His growl went lower.

"How bad do you want to talk to me?"

It was as if he'd somehow hypnotized her and she'd answer any question without reserve.

"Badly."

Gabe slowly straightened, his glittery, angry gaze never leaving hers. The big horse shifted beneath him as if responding to some sort of tension in his rider. Just when she thought he'd decided to ride away and leave her hanging, he spoke.

"Then move your things into my house. If you're still there by supper, I'll eat with you. I'll think about talk—if you've learned enough manners to get through a meal."

And then he rode away. She turned to watch him go, a little stunned to see the horses that had been herded to the tree-shaded pens were now milling inside. The thirty or so animals had trotted past only a few feet away from where she was standing, and it amazed her that she'd neither seen nor heard them or the wranglers who'd brought them in and closed the gate.

Move your things into my house…I'll think about talking if you've learned enough manners…

Tough, uncompromising, but it was as much a warning as it was the chance she'd craved. Gabe Patton would tolerate no misstep or wrong word, and certainly no hint of spite from her ever again. And she didn't know him well enough to know what might set him off, particularly when she was sure that anything, no matter how miniscule or unintended on her part, might well get her thrown out before she even realized what she'd done to rile him.

Mindful that he'd now dismounted and handed his horse off to one of the wranglers and might be about to glance her way, she turned and hurried back to the house, determined to demonstrate that she would immediately comply with his dictates, however more demanding they might become.

And however impossible she feared he could make them.

CHAPTER TWO

GABE PATTON had realized the truth the moment he'd taken the cell call from his housekeeper and heard Lainey's name: His wife was here to divorce him.

Lainey Talbot Patton was the only acquisition he'd not fought to get his hands on or gone to war to keep. Partly because as long as they were married, she was his whether she thought so or not. Partly because he knew she'd been devastated by her father's death and manipulated to within an inch of her life by her harridan mother.

For those first days and weeks after the quick ceremony at the courthouse, Gabe had been amused by her stubbornness and her absolute refusal to allow him any contact with her. But when the days and weeks had turned into months, he'd stopped being amused.

He'd like to credit her mother's death with Lainey's sudden appearance here and her claim to have found out the truth. Her repentant pose had looked startlingly authentic, but they both knew the terms of her father's will, and the fact that she'd waited six months to show up made her apology ring hollow.

According to the terms of the will, Lainey had to stay married to him for five years before she was eligible to receive full control of her inheritance. The five years were almost up, control of Talbot Ranch would revert to her in a few weeks, but her marriage to him—the marriage she'd never given a moment's chance to—would be the only thing standing in her way.

Whatever he'd once hoped they might have together, there was no way in hell he'd just hand over what had been a bankrupt operation to an ungrateful female who'd virtually wiped her feet on him while he'd been risking everything he'd earned to get Talbot Ranch back into the black. Particularly now that she could legally claim control over every inch and dollar of the sweat and risk he'd invested to save it, then maybe make some token thanks before she demanded a divorce.

Though he'd agreed to John's request and would keep their bargain to the letter, he didn't plan to come out of the deal empty-handed.

He glanced toward the main house, but Lainey was no longer in sight. Unless her mother had succeeded in making a hothouse plant of her, he was certain she wouldn't be able to sit around indoors for the rest of the afternoon. He figured she'd go over to Talbot and have a look around, so he didn't let the idea bother him.

Whatever Lainey was up to now, her intention to be free of him wouldn't be as simple as a token apology and a last trip to the courthouse.

Gabe's housekeeper, who introduced herself as Elisa, put Lainey's two suitcases, overnight bag and briefcase in the entry closet just off the front foyer. Uneasy and too restless and keyed up to wait around in the living room for over three hours until supper, Lainey left a hasty note on a paper scrap for Gabe on the coffee table, then left the house.

Her father had been buried in the small family cemetery on Talbot Ranch, so she went there. She drove past the big Victorian house and ranch buildings of the Talbot headquarters, and found the rutted road that stretched through three massive pastures to the gravesite.

The shady acre was enclosed by a white rail fence, and she parked her car outside the painted rails beneath an overhanging tree branch. She went to the trunk for the silk flower arrangement she'd bought in San Antonio, then entered the gate and walked to the headstone that marked John Talbot's grave.

Poignant memories overwhelmed her as she stared at the carved stone and remembered the horror of hearing that her father had been killed. Her desperate race to get back to Texas had been blurred by the shock and numbing grief she'd been certain she couldn't survive, then the terrible agony of his funeral.

How on earth could she have thought her father would do anything to hurt or slight her? For weeks now she'd looked through his pictures again and again, apologizing over and over for ever doubting his love and care for her.

Childish or not, foolish or not, she'd somehow hoped her father had heard her all those times. Perhaps the knowledge of what she'd inflicted on Gabe had prevented her from feeling relief; perhaps self-loathing and guilt would keep her in this torment the rest of her days, whatever Gabe had to say to her tonight.

Quietly she knelt down and placed the silk pansies and forget-me-nots in the slim receptacle at the base of the stone.

"I'm finally home, Daddy."

All the other words crowded up from the love and heartache and brokenness she felt, and poured out in a fresh torrent of sorrow and regret. By the time the torrent had eased away, she had moved to the wrought-iron bench nearby to sit sideways on the end of it to pillow her cheek on the back with her wrists.

The sound of the breeze gently rustling the tree leaves overhead made her aware of its warmth as it brushed lightly over her clothes and teased through her hair. The first true sense of peace she'd felt in years began to trickle through her then, and she remembered the words, *Not a soul on this earth I love more than my baby girl.*

Her father had said that to her frequently, sometimes in his booming voice with a broad smile on his face, sometimes in a moment of gruff sentimentality.

The sweetness of the memory made her whisper back what she always had, "And there's not a soul on this earth your baby girl loves more than her daddy."

Lainey sat there for some time more in the calm that had eluded her for weeks. She'd needed this too long and craved it too desperately to rush away from it now. Drowsy from the heat, she must have dozed until she was roused by what sounded like a faint whisper.

Show him what you're made of...

Half awake, her heart still clinging to the words she must have dreamed, Lainey lifted her head to look past the edge of the trees and note the angle of the sun. Alarm banished her calm and scattered the dreamed whisper. She got quickly to her feet and ran to her car.

Leery of driving too fast on the rutted road, she felt the ominous weight of each frantic second.

Lainey pulled up in front of the Patton main house, switched off the engine, then reached for her handbag and raced to the red doors. She stabbed at the button for the doorbell, then fidgeted as she waited. Elisa opened the door.

"I'm sorry to be late, *señora*. May I come—"

But the woman was already stepping back to graciously wave her inside.

"Do I have time to freshen up?"

"The second door on the hall."

Lainey offered a smile as her heart fell further. The message she read from the way Elisa had answered was that she indeed had no time left, but the woman might have some sympathy for her need to make herself more presentable.

Lainey hurried toward the small bathroom to do something with her hair. She'd used the rearview mirror in her car to help guide her efforts to remove her smudged mascara, then had dug around for hairpins and given her hair a quick brushing, but she still looked wilted and mussed.

Another pass with her brush and a few repairs with the small amount of makeup in her handbag were made more difficult by her shaking hands. It was some consolation that at least Gabe had allowed her into his house.

She had no doubt that Elisa was giving him a report on her disheveled appearance, and she cringed. The last thing she wanted was for Gabe to think she was playing on his sympathy so he'd be nicer to her and perhaps consider forgiving her.

When she'd finished, Lainey found her way to the dining room. She'd never seen the private areas of Gabe's house, but she had been in the main rooms a handful of times years ago. When she reached the formal room, she halted just inside the double doors.

Gabe sat at the head of the long gleaming table, his overlong dark hair still damp from his shower. The jeans and blue-striped shirt he had on were fresh but fairly common. He didn't fuss over his clothes like men who were born to wealth or who worked in offices, and yet there was a quality about him that made him look just as neatly pressed and turned out in work clothes as he did in a suit and tie.

Gabriel Patton was a man who'd grown a substantial income from practically nothing through hard work, careful savvy, and the sheer power of his iron will. He was a man without a college education who'd taken big risks, refused to fail, and whose handshake on a deal made its outcome as certain as the sunrise.

Which was why her wrong beliefs about him had

been such a profound insult to his integrity. This was
a man who'd worked relentlessly to overcome his
hardscrabble upbringing and achieve success. To
even hint that he'd married her out of greed or to
get anything by underhanded means was not only
untrue but morally wrong.

The dark eyes that were too perceptive and too
flat and hard to make her feel even a whisper of
comfort, took note of her sudden entrance. The chill
in his gaze kept her where she was and certainly
didn't show a hint of welcome. She endured it when
his gaze flashed down the front of her to her feet,
but it came back up so suddenly that she thought
she'd imagined the swift look.

"I apologize," she said quickly. "Time got away
from me."

Gabe didn't comment on that, but instead called
his housekeeper in. When Elisa appeared, he simply
glanced her way and she disappeared back into the
kitchen. Then his gaze shifted back to Lainey.

"Might as well sit."

Lainey walked to the place setting to the right of
his. Gabe rose briefly to seat her, but she knew right
away that he did it only because she was a female
guest and he was her host. The fact that he didn't
neglect the courtesy gave her a slim bit of hope.

Elisa brought a tray of food into the silent room
and efficiently set everything out before she re-

treated to the kitchen. Lainey followed Gabe's lead and reached for her napkin.

He didn't speak to her and she didn't feel comfortable trying to speak to him. There was nothing she could conclude about his mood except that it must be dark. He certainly wasn't brimming with eagerness to make conversation with her, so she tried to eat the steak and assortment of vegetables and crusty bread set before her. When the silence bore down too heavily, she found something neutral to say.

"Elisa is an excellent cook."

As if her remark had reminded him that she was sitting at the same table he was, Gabe looked her way. She couldn't bear the searching impact of his gaze, so she looked down at her plate of food and gamely caught a piece of steak with her fork tine.

"You eat like she's poisoned it."

A nervous breath burst out of her before she could stop it. "No, I'm...sorry. My appetite isn't good, but that's not because the food isn't...excellent." She couldn't seem to stop herself from glancing toward him to see his reaction.

As she'd half feared, he was watching her steadily and one of his brows showed a faint curl of both skepticism and curiosity.

"What'd you do?" he asked gruffly. "Get religion?"

The remark felt brutal but she tried not to be discouraged. "I found out what I should have known from the be—"

"Save it."

Subject closed. What little appetite she might have had left flitted away, and she gripped the napkin in her lap with one hand while she tried to force-feed herself the piece of steak with the other. It immediately became difficult to chew, then once she'd got the job done, it was difficult to swallow. She set her fork down and reached for her water glass to take a helpful sip.

And immediately choked on the water. Self-consciousness made it worse, and she covered her mouth with the napkin while the spasms died down. To her relief, Gabe didn't remark on it and never once did she feel the sensation of being stared at.

There were advantages to being ignored and this was one of them. But under the circumstances, Gabe's continued silence, his skepticism and his obvious lack of interest in conversation, seemed to emphasize how little interest he had in any potential apology from her. It was as if he was only biding his time with her, but why? Why put up with her at all if he wasn't interested in the reason she was here or what she had to say?

Lainey made another attempt at her meal, but finally gave up and sat silently, her hands clenched together out of sight in her lap. The mantel clock at the side of the room above the river stone fireplace ticked off the endless seconds. Hundreds of seconds, thousands of them, *billions*.

And then Elisa came in with a small tray of dessert. The pedestal dessert glasses were filled with chocolate mousse and topped with a crinkly dollop of whipped cream. Chilled, the outside of the stout glasses were already beginning to fog over as Elisa removed Lainey's picked over plate and replaced it with the dessert.

Normally the treat was Lainey's favorite, but her appetite reacted no better to the sight of it than it had to the fine meal. Nevertheless, she couldn't refuse it so she picked up her spoon to dig in. At least the mousse would slide down more easily than the steak and vegetables had.

She'd managed two bites before the rich chocolate flavor touched off her appetite. Focused on the rich dessert, she was able to keep from glancing toward Gabe. But then she heard a soft sound of movement and glanced his way in time to see him lift his untouched chocolate and set it next to the one she'd nearly finished.

"Fill in those empty places," he said, his voice low and gravelly with a kind of masculine gentleness that caught her off guard and sent a tidal wave of emotion through her.

"But don't you—"

"Your favorite, not mine."

His dark gaze was probing again, but with less force than before. Now it dawned on her that he might have made a special request to Elisa to prepare the dessert. If so, why had he been so harsh with her during the meal? Was this sudden generosity some sort of apology?

Leery of rejecting what might at least be a small offering of thoughtfulness, she made herself murmur a soft thanks. She'd eat the second dessert if it killed her. Though it went down slower than the first one, she managed the task but when it was gone, she set her spoon down and waited tensely for what would happen next.

"Elisa's taken our coffee to the den."

Lainey's momentary relief that the meal was finally done was swallowed up by renewed anxiety as she eased back her chair to stand. Apparently Gabe meant to let her have the talk she wanted, but now that the time had come, she was back to worrying that he'd reject everything she had to say.

Lainey stood and then paused, glancing up at him. "I need to get my briefcase."

The dark flicker in his gaze held hers. "If it's papers, I'm not interested." The dark flicker vanished because his gaze shifted and he waited for her to precede him out of the room. Once they were through the doors she hesitated, not certain where the room was.

As if he'd remembered that, Gabe directed her along the edge of the large living room to a hall in the east wing that brought them quickly to the den. French doors on the outside wall opened to a wide patio that was ringed with enough trees to shade the patio stones in the heat of the day.

All the other walls in the room were lined floor to ceiling with built-in bookcases. Among the books and stock magazines neatly stored on the many shelves were Native American artifacts and pieces of cowboy art. The furniture was heavy and masculine, and a few brightly colored Mexican throw rugs lay on the floor atop a carpet made up of a small variety of dark shades that wouldn't show much of what might get tracked in during a workday.

Lainey might have felt comfortable in the large room and taken several minutes to more closely examine several of the pieces in the bookcases if anyone but Gabe had owned the room. Hesitantly she sat down on one of the two leather wing chairs he indicated in front of the big desk. The coffee tray was on the small table between her chair and his, so she looked over at him as he was sitting down.

"Pour for both of us, if you like," he said, and settled back to watch her fill their cups.

She handed the first cup to him, then poured one for herself to soothe her dry mouth. When she'd finished, she slid back only slightly in the big chair to take a sip before she set the cup back down on the table. Weary of the wait but so anxious about it that she was on the verge of losing her nerve, she plunged in.

"I'm not sure where to start, but there are several things you deserve to hear."

Now she braved a look at him and saw him leaning back calmly, studying her face. "Start with your plans for July."

The gravelly request caught her off guard. He'd made it sound like a request, though he'd worded it as a demand. July was the month they'd been married five years ago. According to her father's will, July was the month that sole control of Talbot Ranch would revert to her if she'd stayed married to Gabe for a full five years.

"I'm not here about who'll control Talbot Ranch or what will happen in July with this marriage. I'm here to apologize and, if you're interested, to explain why I've acted the way I have."

"I'm not interested in pretty apologies. What I'm interested in are your plans for July. Will you file for divorce?"

Lainey couldn't mistake the iron will beneath his words. Or the fine thread of anger mixed in. But why would divorce even be a question after what she'd done to him all these years? As far as she was concerned, divorce was a given. What Gabe didn't know was that she'd found out about what he'd done for Talbot Ranch and she planned to do something about it.

"I've just recently found out that Talbot Ranch was virtually bankrupt when you took over," she began, "and it looks like you saved it single-handedly in spite of what I did to you. I suspect you covered my inheritance taxes out of your own pocket when I thought they'd come from my father's investments."

She paused, but his stony expression told her nothing. "And since the quarterly checks I thought were from profits due me from Talbot Ranch must also have been paid out of your private accounts, I owe you a substantial amount of money in addition to a complete apology."

Lainey finished briskly with, "On the subject of July, I'm certain you can't possibly want to stay married a second longer than you agreed to."

"Why's that?"

The sudden comeback was unexpected, and she sat there a moment until she realized why. This was the opening for her to finally make the "pretty apology" he kept referring to so skeptically.

"As I've said—"

"I made a *vow*," he said, bluntly cutting her off, "'till death do us part.'"

The quiet words were like a sudden blow and Lainey felt the punch so vividly that it stole her breath. Her brain registered the shock, then she felt a new one when she belatedly realized the significance of what he'd just said.

I made a vow…

A vow made by a man whose handshake was as dependable as the sunrise; a vow made by a man whose words could be carved in granite and put in a museum.

Till death do us part…

"Surely you didn't…" Her voice trailed away as the breathless feeling affected her again. "There's no reason for you to sacrifice…"

The right words wouldn't seem to come to her, but however shocked and rattled she was by what he'd said, Gabe was sitting back comfortably, his dark eyes intense as he watched everything about her and appeared to be waiting for her to finish what she was struggling to say.

"It was a marriage yes, but not a *real* marriage," she tried again. "A—a business deal to help protect my inheritance, not a real…marriage?" The question she'd subconsciously put on the word invited an answer she hadn't wanted to ask—didn't want!— and her nerves began to jump and twist and scream.

Gabe seemed to know all that, so he let the wild silence stretch before he spoke, and the wait seemed to underscore every word that fell on her like the blow of a rock chisel on that museum-worthy piece of granite.

"No business deal I've ever made came with a

'till death' pledge before a judge,'' he drawled in a low, rough voice, "or a wedding ring. Or a woman's signature next to mine on a marriage license."

The flash of heat that went through her all the way from her hairline to her feet scrambled her brain. She tried to think of something to say to that, some way to counter the grim statement he'd just made.

"You can't mean that—you can't really want me." Another thought saved her and she added hastily, "Is this a way to get back at me for…what I've done to you all these years?"

She stared at him in the long silence while shock after shock thrummed through her and pounded home the knowledge that Gabriel Patton really did aim to stay married to her. There was no mistaking the flinty look in his eyes as anything but resolve.

"What did you think I was supposed to get?" he asked then, and she felt her heart quiver.

She sealed her lips firmly together, loathe to say the words *a wife*. And he hadn't answered her question about getting back at her.

"I was denied the benefits and privileges of the five year marriage I agreed to make," he went on in that same low, gravelly drawl that suddenly seemed more masculine growl than speech. "The deal I made wasn't satisfied."

Her heart began to flutter quicker and quicker. An even worse nightmare than facing Gabe and enduring whatever awful things he might say to her, was to face him and hear *this*.

"I'm sorry for that," she said hoarsely, "but it's—it's not realistic to think that staying married for another five years will satisfy anything."

"Have you made plans with another man?"

She couldn't help the flush of heat that surged into her face. "Of course not."

"So the man your mother chose for you didn't make it past dinner?"

The flush of heat suddenly became a scorching mask and the guilt she already felt about that subject bore down more heavily. "If you know about him, then you know there was nothing but dinner. Ever. And there were two other couples present."

Lainey couldn't bear the stern gaze that stared fixedly into hers as if trying to see the truth, but she didn't dare look away. She should rail at him for hiring an investigator to spy on her, but after what she'd done to shut him so completely out of her life, she could hardly blame him.

Thank God she'd done nothing that could be considered unfaithful, but the fact that Gabe had known about it deepened her shame. She'd never been romantically attracted to the man her mother had coerced her into having dinner with, and she'd felt so guilty about that one time that she'd never let Sondra maneuver her into another date with anyone else.

"I shouldn't have gone out with anyone for any reason," she admitted quietly. "I apologize for that, too."

"So you'd have no distractions while you live up to your vows?"

Lainey stared at him helplessly. As intense as her crush on Gabe had once been, he'd been mostly a stranger to her. And now he was not only still a stranger, but a stranger who would naturally feel no small amount of ill will toward her. She'd be a fool to give him a chance like that. He could make mincemeat of her.

"I don't think that's what either of us really wants," she said shakily.

"There's no 'us' in that. Just you."

The way he'd said "just you" somehow emphasized what he didn't say: she'd gotten all the benefits of her father's will—what would actually amount to several million dollars worth of benefits—without giving Gabe a single thing in exchange but trouble and public embarrassment. It was obvious he didn't consider her offer of financial compensation to be enough to satisfy him.

But she had to remember that everyone in their part of Texas had known that they'd married, so it followed that everyone had to have noticed that she'd never lived a moment with Gabe as his wife. And because neither of them had ever lived as hermits, the gossip about them must have been intense.

She'd let old friendships drift to protect herself from hearing it, but Gabe had lived here knowing it was swirling around him, though she doubted anyone would have dared to repeat it to his face.

The guilt she'd felt these last weeks was suddenly nothing compared to the guilt she felt now. Nausea rose like a tidal wave as she felt the jaws of a trap snap tighter and tighter on her conscience.

Because she'd deprived Gabe of the marriage he'd bargained for, he was insisting that she live up to her vows and continue it. But the idea was terrifying. It wasn't possible to have a normal marriage with him now, not after five whole years of hateful estrangement.

"Please, Gabe," she croaked, but he spoke almost before she'd finished saying the short syllable of his name.

"I want heirs."

CHAPTER THREE

HEIRS...

Lainey felt the room tip and she sat back deeper in the chair to steady herself. He meant children. *More than one.*

One child was beyond comprehension, but more than one was mind-blowing. She'd been staring at Gabe, but she hadn't really been seeing his stony expression or the no-nonsense glitter in his eyes. She'd been staring at the sudden mental flash of children. Beautiful dark-haired toddlers with dark eyes...more than one toddler, more than two...at intervals of not much more than a year or two apart.

Gabe's gruff voice made the picture fade.

"If you'd stayed, you could have done your part in Talbot's comeback. We'd be playin' with our babies tonight."

Gabe's stony expression was tempered by a faint softening in his gaze when he'd said *our babies* that was gone the second after it showed. She'd almost missed it.

After a lifetime with her mother Lainey recognized emotional manipulation, but this wasn't precisely that because it was the simple truth. If she'd stayed, she had no doubt things would have worked out somehow.

After all, though her heart had been filled with silly adolescent fantasies about Gabe that no flesh-and-blood man could ever live up to, she'd once thought he was the only man she'd ever love. If she'd not been so shocked by her father's death and hurt by his will, having Gabriel Patton handed to her so easily would have been the fulfillment of her fondest romantic hope.

So yes, they could have been playing with their children tonight in peace. The question of what happened in July or the state of their marriage would have long since been determined.

Her father would have expected his daughter to pull her own weight in both the saving of Talbot Ranch and her marriage. The fact that he hadn't spelled it out in the will made Lainey realize her father had taken her respect for his wishes and her integrity so for granted that he'd seen no reason to insult her by putting those specifics in writing.

If it was possible, her regret over it all deepened into a heavier feeling of heartsickness than ever. The brief glimpse of softness in Gabe's eyes just now when he'd mentioned babies impacted her in a new way then.

Of course Gabe Patton would want a family. He didn't have any now, and hadn't since he'd been in his midteens. He'd been nearing his late twenties when he'd married her, so he was at least thirty-two or thirty-three by now. It shamed her to realize she didn't remember his birth date, but what nicked her heart was the reminder that he'd been waiting a long time to have someone to share his life with.

She'd not only deprived him of that, but his marriage to her had prevented him from finding someone more worthy to marry.

Lainey stared over at him, helpless to look away from this self-sufficient, sometimes arrogant man who was so tough and hard-edged. There was no reason, just by looking at him, to think anything could hurt him or that there was anything soft or vulnerable in him at all. And yet she felt it suddenly, in spite of his harshness.

Her father had respected Gabe and admired what he'd achieved, and Gabe had considered his much older neighbor a trusted friend. Neither man could have seriously figured the will would be needed. John Talbot had simply taken a precaution to safeguard Lainey against her mother's manipulations until she'd had time to achieve full independence from Sondra's demands and returned to Talbot Ranch. She was certain now, knowing her father, that he would have dropped the conditions on her inheritance the moment she had.

In the meantime, he must have expected to re-

cover Talbot wealth himself but before he could get
very far, his sudden death had saddled Gabe with a
commitment to both a rebellious wife and a monumental financial challenge.

And of course, that rebellious wife had stupidly
abandoned it all to him.

Somehow Lainey found the courage to ask, "If
you knew Talbot was bankrupt before we went
through with the ceremony, why didn't you just refuse to marry me? You could surely tell by then that
I didn't deserve to get anything, much less waste a
moment of your time."

Belatedly she remembered that Gabriel Patton
didn't operate that way. His word was the law he
lived by. Whether she'd deserved anything wasn't
the issue. He'd given his word.

She shrank inwardly from the unintentional insult
and rushed out with, "I didn't ask the question to
offend you." The tense silence didn't last long.

"Your daddy trusted me to look out for you in
case he couldn't," he said somberly, but she saw no
sign that her question had bothered him. "A man
works all his life to leave something he's proud of
for his kids and his kids' kids. John wanted you to
keep every acre and dime of Talbot."

Emotion virtually choked her as she sensed the
deeper part of what he'd said. Just as John Talbot
had wanted to pass on his life's work to her, Gabriel

Patton would want to pass on what he'd built to his children. The only inheritance he'd gotten had been an old saddle and a box of clothes.

He'd bargained for a wife and children of his own and she'd thwarted that. She'd doomed any chance of happiness they might have had, and it was only fair to not tie up any more of Gabe's time. There were multitudes of women more worthy of him than she was.

"You've seen what I can be like," she tried again. "I'm sure the last thing that makes sense is for you to have children with a woman who's behaved as I have."

She felt a small quiver of hope because she'd made what she thought was a sound point, since there could be no way now for their marriage to work. But Gabe spoke again and somehow his words made it even more impossible for her to think of wiggling out of this.

"Today you said you were sorry, that you'd grovel if that's what it took." His stony expression didn't change by so much as the faintest shadow. "Easy to say."

He rose from his chair then walked around the desk to the French doors behind it that opened onto the patio. He stopped a moment to take down his black Stetson from where he'd upended it on a nearby shelf, then reached for the door lever.

"I'll be out till full dark. I reckon we'll find out quick whether you take after John or Sondra."

Gabe opened the door and only then did he look back at her. His dark eyes glittered with something Lainey wasn't sure she could define at first as anything but cool intensity.

But everywhere his gaze wandered in that scattering of seconds, heat trailed over her skin. It was a look that was blatantly possessive. Whatever he'd said about who she "took after," she sensed this wasn't the end for him, whatever she chose to do. Any doubt about that was instantly made clear.

"We would have shared the same bed on our wedding night," he said, his low drawl so quiet and gruff that it was almost smoky. "If your word means anything now, tell Elisa to put your things where I sleep."

If Lainey had been standing, she would have fainted. As it was, it was a miracle she didn't fall out of her chair. She stared, dazed as he went out and pulled the door closed behind him before he stepped away from the glass to start in the direction of the barns.

She could barely get a full breath as she felt the fresh weight of Gabe's expectations fall on her like hundred-pound rocks.

If your word means anything...

It was a last chance to live up to her father's final

wish and fulfill her obligation to Gabe. The miserable knowledge made her feel as if she was being dragged down a steep incline toward what could only be the deadly cliff edge of a straight drop to disaster.

Lainey had been racking her brain for weeks to think of a way to make up for what she'd done. She'd been willing to do anything, *anything,* to atone and to demonstrate to Gabe that she was truly sorry.

She'd planned to hire a team to comb through the records of everything Gabe had spent and done to bring Talbot back so she could make him a fair financial offer to reimburse him. She'd been thinking in terms of money or land, but she'd never dreamed he'd want *this.*

Tell Elisa to put your things where I sleep.

Something completely feminine began to pulse deep inside that was a sensual mix of excitement, terror and thrill. The fantasies she'd had about Gabe from the time she was almost eighteen until her father had died when she was almost twenty, surged forcefully.

The dark, possessive look Gabe had just given her made it impossible not to entertain thoughts of what it might be like to go through with their marriage, to sleep in his bed tonight with the expectations he must surely have about what would happen there.

But those were expectations Lainey could in no way fulfill. Neither of them truly knew each other and she wasn't certain of Gabe, however dependable his word was. And he couldn't possibly love her. Indeed he might never be able to love her after she'd gone so far over the line.

It was then that she realized how utterly worn out she was from all the horrors and fears and regrets that had battered and tormented her for so many endless weeks. And now all of them were rising to heights she'd never dreamed of.

Lainey only briefly considered what turning Gabe down would do for her peace of mind, then finally stood and walked reluctantly toward the door to the hall.

He was right. It was one thing to say the words and believe you meant them, but quite another thing entirely if someone expected you to live up to them. Hadn't she somehow known, despite trying to talk Gabe out of this, that she'd end up complying with his expectations?

She went to Elisa before she lost her nerve, but she'd go in search of Gabe afterward. Whatever he'd mandated for tonight, there had to be some way to win a promise from him that there'd be no intimacies between them before they could get to know each other. Perhaps if she could make Gabe understand that she was willing to go through with this marriage, he'd back away from his demand that she share his bed from the first night.

The sun was still an hour or more from setting by the time she'd washed her feet and put on her boots for the walk to the barns. She eventually found Gabe in the colt pasture with the dozen or so weaned colts that had crowded around him.

The sight of Gabe patiently touching or giving a calm rub to each of the youngsters reminded her of something she'd always admired about him. Gabe was good with any kind of animal, especially horses. He was uncommonly patient with them and had a knack for gaining their trust.

He never tolerated abuse. Lainey and her father had been here on Patton Ranch the day a new ranch hand had beaten a horse with a gate chain because it had been startled by the start up of a tractor. Gabe had fired the man on the spot and only just managed to keep himself from using the piece of chain on the ranch hand.

A man who could be outraged by the mistreatment of an animal yet had the self-control to keep from doing violence, was surely a man who was in control of his emotions and passionate urges. It helped a little to realize that.

Gabe must have known she was coming the moment she entered the pasture because the colts' attention had turned her way, but he ignored her approach until she'd almost reached him.

The colts milled a bit when she joined them, and then a handful of velvety noses pressed toward her to give curious inspections. Lainey moved slowly and petted some of the bolder ones before she glanced at Gabe and caught him watching her.

"I was wondering if you'd consider going on with this a bit slower," she started, a little amazed that she'd kept the nervous tremor out of her voice. She saw the subtle tightening of the stern line of his mouth but went on.

"I told Elisa precisely what you said, to show my good faith. Since I did, I hoped perhaps you might consider letting me use the bedroom that connects yours. Until we're a bit more...comfortable with each other."

Gabe had watched her quietly but when she finished, he spoke.

"I've never forced myself on a woman and I'll not start with my wife."

The gruff words touched her in a sweetly peculiar way and she sensed a rare masculine tenderness beneath his rugged surface. It somehow hinted at both need and a shocking vulnerability, but surely she was projecting onto him the things she'd want in any husband. Lainey tried to ignore it and go on.

"We're virtual strangers," she said softly, "and

this is the first night we'll spend beneath the same roof."

The tenderness she thought she'd seen in him fled as an implacable gleam came into his eyes, though it was in no way harsh.

"Start as you mean to go. Works well with the stock and hired help. Ought to work with wives."

The blunt words almost startled a nervous laugh out of her, but the need to object to them overcame the reaction.

"Maybe," she conceded, careful to not sound confrontational. "But you aren't out here putting a saddle on these colts," she pointed out. "Though they're too young, you also know they need time to get used to you and develop some sort of affec— trust—toward you."

His stony expression didn't change. "You want me to pet you, handle your feet and run my hands all over you like I do the colts?"

Heat flashed into her face as she prudently avoided a direct reply to that. "Those aren't the first things you do, because I've watched you before. First you coax them close, but you move slow, *very* slow. You've never forced or crowded them. You wait and slowly persuade. When they come to you, and they do, they think it's their idea."

Relief began to ease through her then. She'd made a valid point in a way that she was certain Gabe, as a man who knew instinctively how to win animals over, could relate to.

His stony expression gentled the tiniest bit. "You aren't a baby anymore, Ms. Lainey." That slow, smoky quality had come back into his low voice. "You were at twenty, but you're five years down the road now."

Lainey was suddenly breathless because she sensed what was coming. He didn't make her wait.

"When a grown horse that's never been handled or worked comes in, it's best to start on 'em right away. Years of training to make up for, and since an adult horse is capable of being put under a saddle within a half hour, there's no reason to delay making him useful. He never gets time to develop a habit of being aimless in the company of humans. Or spoiled."

It was amazing how easily he'd usurped her analogy and smoothly turned it back on her. She could tell by the sudden glitter in his eyes that there was more.

"I've been a long time without sex, Mrs. Patton," he said bluntly. "Years."

The candid declaration shocked her, but the word *years* reached for her and sent a bolt of sensual heat through her insides. Suddenly she felt dizzy and weak. Her shock must have shown because the glitter in his eyes intensified. She knew instantly that what he'd read in her expression had offended him.

His voice was a growl. "I reckon I've still got some self-control left now that the drought is nearer an end."

"I don't mean to suggest that you're some kind of—"

"The days start earlier out here than they do in the big city," Gabe cut in as he nodded in the direction of the house. "Best you get ready for an early night before I come in."

Lainey stared at him in disbelief as he turned away. Oh, God, she'd just made things worse between them, and she hurried after him as he walked to the pasture fence.

"I'm sorry, Gabe. I just seem to keep saying the wrong things."

He kept walking, a few of the colts trailing along to keep up with them, but his harsh profile showed no hint of softening. She tried again.

"I'm trying to say that we're strangers. I'm not opposed to...sharing your room, but I naturally feel awkward about it so soon. Surely you feel the same way? You don't know me either, and what you know hasn't been good. It can't make you feel comfortable to think about sleeping next to me."

"Are you dangerous?" That came out in another

growl, but he didn't spare her so much as a brief glance.

"Well, no, of course not. But even without our history, we're strangers."

His profile was still set. "That'll change tonight. And tomorrow and the next night and all the days and nights to come."

They'd reached the pasture gate. Lainey was so frustrated and intimidated by his ongoing edicts that she didn't know whether to scream or cry. Gabe unhooked the chain to open the gate enough to let her walk through the narrow space ahead of him. She quickly did, then waited for him to secure the latch and set the chain in place.

Once he had, he looked down at her, his stony, no-nonsense expression unrelenting. "You best get on up to the house."

Though delivered softly, it was an even stronger dismissal than the first one, and Lainey could tell he took a dim view of having to repeat it. It was also a not so subtle message that the subject of where he expected her to sleep tonight was firmly closed, though what she did about it—considering his wishes on the subject—was now up to her.

Which essentially gave her no choice if she was sincere about living up to her long-delayed obligation to him, and they both knew it.

Lainey took a step back, hesitating as she hoped

for any sign that he might change his mind before she turned and walked to the house. Every step she took pounded home the reminder that this was part of the consequence for what she'd done to Gabe, but was there any hope that she could eventually pay in full?

Show him what you're made of...

Whether she'd dreamed the sound of her father's voice saying those words today or not, it was clear that living up to her vows with Gabe, on his terms now, was the only way to settle her debt.

Lainey saw the benefit of taking her shower and preparing for bed before Gabe came back to the house. She would have felt even more self-conscious if he'd been waiting in the bedroom outside the master bath, able to hear her go through her nighttime routine.

She'd thought over everything Gabe had said and done this afternoon and evening at least a dozen times. Though he seemed deadly serious about her living up to the marriage vows she'd taken with him, she couldn't get away from the notion that this whole thing might very well be simple revenge to get back at her before he divorced her anyway.

She wondered once again why a self-sufficient man like Gabe, who claimed he took his ''till death'' vows so seriously, would ever make a commitment to a woman he didn't love, one he'd not been certain could ever love him. Particularly when a man like him could have had his pick of women.

The answer hit her like a lightning strike: because of the bitter way he'd grown up and the utterly driven way Gabe had made something of himself, perhaps he'd not had time for the soft, civilizing social rituals that other men had passed through in their adolescence and early adulthood.

Her marriage to Gabe had put a damper on her own social habits, because it had stopped the dating she'd done in school and after graduation. She'd at least gone through the social ritual of having young men show up for dates and proms who'd brought corsages or flowers, and endured her father's "private words" with them before allowing her to go out with them.

But who had Gabe ever been seen going out with? Lainey mentally raced to remember. She'd heard tawdry gossip at some point before he'd bought his ranch and also in the early years of ownership, that Gabe had only gone out with women who'd been savvy enough to know he might not have much money for classy restaurants; women who'd chased him anyway because he was so compellingly macho.

Women who'd apparently reacted to him in a sexual way, but who didn't care that he'd had very little or that he'd sweated and dirtied his hands for a living, because something about him had thrilled them until some richer, easier man had come along. Later, after Gabe had sweated himself into a fortune, they'd come after him again, but this time as a meal ticket. Her father had remarked on that part more than once.

Perhaps the opportunity to get a wife he considered suitable without risking the social delicacies of actual courtship had seemed pragmatic and ideal to him, and preferable to running a gauntlet of gold diggers.

Gabe was so much harder and no-nonsense than he'd been years ago, so perhaps he preferred even more the efficiency and lack of emotion such a marriage match would make.

Lainey hoped he'd actually courted at least one nice woman chastely with flowers and formality over a period of time. If all he'd ever done was run with oversexed women who didn't mind one-night stands—or who'd slept with him a few times before moving on to someone with more money—Gabe might have more carnal notions about what ''getting to know each other better'' meant.

Whatever Gabe's reasons for marrying her in the beginning, the fact was she'd shamed him and everyone knew it. His pride had taken blow after blow, and though she honestly and bitterly regretted it now, it would be just deserts if he turned the tables and dealt her a strong taste of public humiliation.

Dread made her increase her pace in the nervous circle she walked in the open space of the large bedroom. It was impossible for her to think they could ever trust each other. Still perpetually obsessed by the guilt of what she'd done, Lainey wondered again whether it was safe to risk that Gabe would somehow avenge himself on her, or whether she should just grab her things and run back to Chicago.

Surely her lawyer could untangle the mess she'd made of both her inheritance and her marriage. Though she'd doomed the marriage even before they'd taken vows, it was only right that Gabe was fairly compensated for what he'd done to save Talbot Ranch, if not receive the lion's share of her inheritance.

And if she gave him the lion's share, what would she ever want with perhaps only the main house and a few acres when she might never have the courage to live there and face everyone after what she'd done? Because she already owed Gabe a vast fortune, it might be more efficient to just let every bit of it go to him.

Nerves and exhaustion intensified everything. Since she couldn't seem to stop fretting over it all on her own, Lainey was almost relieved when she heard Gabe's bootsteps on the flat stones outside the

French doors that opened from the master bedroom onto the patio.

Taking a hasty second to tightly cinch the belt of her silk robe securely over her pajamas, she stopped pacing and turned toward the doors when she heard the click of the latch. Belatedly she realized she should have opened the heavy drapes enough for him to get in.

Lainey rushed toward the doors to at least catch the edge of the drape and move it out of the way, but Gabe easily dealt with it himself and came in. Lainey stopped halfway to him and gripped her hands together to keep them from visibly trembling. It wouldn't be a good idea to insult him with a show of nervousness.

Gabe closed the door and let the drape fall back into place before he looked over at her. The distant chime of the grandfather clock in the living room marked the ten o'clock hour and reminded Lainey that it was much later than just after dark.

And much later for her than she'd feared.

CHAPTER FOUR

THE glittery look in Gabe's eyes softened into smoldering heat as his gaze took note of her brushed hair and then trailed slowly over her from face to bare toes. It was a look that missed no detail, and left her feeling as if he'd put his hands in every place that it lingered.

"What do you call that color?"

The trivial question threw her. "The salesclerk called it gold, but I think it's a little too yellow to be...gold." She tried not to let her dismay over her babbling answer show.

"That the only kind of nightclothes you brought with you?"

Lainey hadn't given a thought to her full-length pajamas and the long robe, but the outfit was probably more modest and concealing than most husbands would prefer. Particularly a husband who seemed determined to make up for lost time.

"I usually wear this style."

"Next time we're in San Antonio, we'll shop for something more...womanish."

Lainey glanced down. She'd never considered her

preference for pajamas over gowns as being less than feminine. Or less than "womanish."

"A man likes his woman to wear a little lace and ribbon for him in private."

Lainey looked up. His candid remarks suggested not only a very male craving for womanly softness, but a deep appreciation of femininity. They also hinted faintly at the vulnerability she kept sensing beneath his tough guy exterior.

"You gonna ask me again about the other bedroom?"

The sudden switch was another surprise. His dark gaze held hers as he reached up to take off his Stetson. She gripped her fingers together more tightly.

"Do you want me to?"

As if it was such a regular habit that he no longer thought about it consciously, Gabe upended the Stetson on the wing chair set at the side of the French doors as he said, "No, ma'am, I do not."

The gravelly softness of his low voice and his use of "ma'am," made her feel warm toward him. He was suddenly not a dictator issuing edicts, but a hard man who'd set aside a little of his complexity to be a bit more approachable.

She sensed the subtle invitation to closeness in the softening of his gaze. It was almost as if he knew precisely how hard it was for her to think about sharing his bed tonight, so he might be thinking of some way to reassure her somehow, though they both knew he'd never back down on the subject of where she'd sleep.

Did he really want to make her feel a little more comfortable, or was she just so nervous about tonight that she was imagining this?

The earthy masculinity that must have lured dozens of females to him reached across the distance between them to lure her. Lainey had never been immune to Gabe, however much she'd denied it these past years.

For the very first time it dawned on her that all that earthy masculinity was now focused on her, as if it was naturally compelled to seize and possess any female in close range. Gabe was determined to have the full benefit of this marriage, so that was probably the reason for his sudden intensity.

Lainey already understood completely that, at best, she herself was secondary to his real goal, and merely the necessary means to an end. She was in no way the choice of his heart.

And yet, with his dark gaze virtually devouring her, it was difficult to remember that Gabriel Patton would have stared like this at any woman he'd married. Or that he would have undertaken this exact same campaign with any wife he'd made vows with to both thwart a divorce and to lay claim to the heirs he'd bargained to get.

Because Gabe continued to stand where he was as if he was waiting for her to make some move, the air between them suddenly crackled with expectation. Just as she decided that she was too tired to be reading him clearly and should ignore the kinder impressions that she saw so little outward evidence of, he spoke.

"Maybe if you'd greet your husband the way a wife does when he comes to the house, you'd be more at ease."

The comment jangled her. Would he continually put her on the spot? Was this a bit of the revenge she was worried about or a sign of his impatience about having to wait for full intimacy?

Or could it simply be the no-frills shortcut of a pragmatic, no-nonsense tough guy who wasn't content to wait for nature to take its course? Had he said it because he so rarely allowed his emotions to dictate his actions that he was prompting her not to be governed by them either?

For all Gabe's patience with animals this, besides everything else, suggested he meant to pressure her into compliance at every opportunity rather than patiently waiting for things between them to develop at a prudent pace.

Whatever comeuppance she deserved for all the

things she'd done to Gabe and deprived him of, she didn't want to start the physical part of their marriage with coldhearted compliance. Somehow she scraped up the nerve to let him know that.

"Wouldn't you rather there was genuine feeling behind it," she asked quietly, "or is this truly only about sex and heirs?"

"Won't be about anything but those things if there's no honest try for more."

His dark gaze searched hers and she suddenly got a new impression. Could this tough, no-nonsense man who seemed to set such small store by emotion, have entertained a fantasy or two about how things were between husbands and wives? Surely not, but there was no way to mistake the hint of something almost yearning in the way he'd worded it.

Maybe if you'd greet your husband the way a wife does when he comes to the house…

He extended a big hand toward her, and his gruff voice softened to that deep, smoky quality. "Come here, Lainey."

Something very vulnerable and feminine in her began to quake with both terror and dark excitement. As if his hand was somehow a magnet she couldn't resist or escape, she started hesitantly forward.

And then she felt silly for the fear she felt. What he wanted was harmless. He didn't seem to expect her to go the whole way, just that she greet him as a wife would a husband who'd just come into the house. That didn't mean he wanted her to climb all over him or that he would climb all over her. Surely a casual wifely greeting wasn't such a big deal.

It was one thing to think that and another thing to believe it, but Lainey walked all the way to him and put her hand in his before she eased closer still and placed her other hand on his shoulder to urge him to bend down. The feel of his calloused hand and the rocklike muscle beneath his blue-striped shirt sent an earthquake through every feminine place.

He was a giant compared to her own five-foot-seven frame, but it was amazing that when he began to lean down in an instant response to her very light touch, she felt like the strongest, most powerful woman in the world.

Their gazes meshed and she felt a fresh series of small earthquakes deep down as his warm breath gusted lightly on her face. At the last second she turned coward, and instead of the kiss of lips he must have been waiting for, she shifted slightly to kiss his lean cheek.

His free hand came around her waist and she realized she was little more than an inch from touching him from chest to knee. Her legs went dangerously weak as the heat from his body penetrated her clothes, and she couldn't move. Gabe lifted his head slightly and again stared deep into her eyes. To her relief he showed no trace of impatience or disappointment.

"You smell as beautiful as you look tonight," he murmured, his low voice carrying a burr of sincerity that landed sweetly on her heart. The hand at her back rubbed slightly over the elegant silk of her robe and she felt a shower of hot tingles radiate through her from the small movement. She couldn't seem to speak, not even to come up with some sort of thanks for his compliment.

"I take it back about your nightclothes not being womanish. They feel smooth and warm against you, maybe the way your bare skin will feel. A man likes the feel of his woman's skin even better than ribbons and lace."

The blunt words spoken the way he'd said them were somehow lavishly sensual. As if he couldn't get enough of the feel of the costly silk that concealed the soft flesh beneath, his wide palm continued to press ever so gently against her back while his hard fingers moved in slow circles that made her think he prized the sensation of silk over skin. The small movements were hypnotic.

He guided the fingers she'd placed in his other hand to his chest then eased that arm around her, too. And yet he didn't move her so much as a fraction of an inch closer. The strong, steady cadence of his heart beneath her palm made her even more aware of the sensuality that wrapped around them in gauzy layer after sweet, gauzy layer.

So slowly she didn't register it at first, he bent toward her, his gaze still holding her immovable as once again she felt his warm breath feather over her face. He came so close that her eyes fell shut, but more because she didn't seem to have the power to keep them open than because she meant to close them.

She was so breathless now, so completely paralyzed by the notion that he was about to kiss her, that the milliseconds seemed achingly long.

And then his hard mouth eased gently against hers. A profound wave of emotion swept through her as his lips finessed hers so lightly and thoroughly that she felt, rather than merely sensed, the great tenderness in him.

Gabe was so big and rugged, so hard and implacable, that the contrast between that and this exquisite tenderness beguiled her.

And then the kiss ended as softly as it had begun. It had been little more than a tantalizing taste, but a tantalizing taste that made her incapable of breathing properly. Somehow Lainey managed to open her eyes to watch his slow retreat.

"Best we get some sleep."

His voice was gruff again, and the subject of kissing and their few moments of sensuality and closeness were suddenly as closed from sight and sensation as if they had been padlocked away in a distant room. Gabe released her to step away and cross to the huge walk-in closet. Lainey turned to watch him go, still a little dazed and off-kilter. Had she done something wrong? Had he been disappointed?

Gabe didn't close the door to the big closet, and she could see inside as he pried off his boots on the bootjack then began to unbutton his shirt. He was facing the row of clothes on one of the clothes rods, so she was seeing him from the side as his shirt came off and she saw the spectacular muscle-definition of his bared shoulders and arms and torso.

When he reached for his belt buckle, she realized how matter-of-factly he undressed, fully aware that the door was open and that she was watching, but as unconcerned about it as if they'd lived as man and wife for years.

Lainey turned away and walked shakily to the bed to draw down the comforter and top sheet. She heard the door to the master bath close and knew Gabe had finished undressing. He'd probably come to bed in a few minutes, so this might be her last opportunity to take off her robe and slip beneath the covers while he wasn't in the room to see. Now that those fleeting moments of sensuality and closeness had been taken away so abruptly, she was more self-conscious than ever.

The moment Lainey chose the side opposite the French doors and climbed into Gabe's massive bed, she realized she didn't know which side he preferred.

It was then that something else dawned on her: she knew he'd undressed, but she'd not been aware of any sound that had indicated he had put on anything else. Surely he'd sleep in something tonight whether he normally did or not.

Lainey covered up and stared uneasily at the ceiling a few moments while she listened to water run in the bathroom. Weeks of unrelenting emotional turmoil had drained her and, despite her nervousness, her eyelids felt impossibly heavy now that she was lying down. The drugging pull of exhaustion smothered her tension and she suddenly didn't care about anything but sleep.

Surely Gabe would simply come to bed, turn off the light, then roll away from her and go to sleep. She no longer worried whether he was dressed or not, because she was wearing full-length pajamas buttoned to her chin and he'd already agreed to wait for intimacy. The way he'd turned so indifferent after he'd rocked her with that kiss surely meant that there'd be nothing more tonight.

And that tender kiss a few minutes ago couldn't

truly count much toward the kind of intimacy she
hoped to delay, since it had been surprisingly chaste.
Reassured by that, Lainey dozed off so swiftly and
effortlessly that she didn't know when the door to
the master bathroom opened.

Lainey had fallen deeply asleep. Gabe could tell by
the complete absence of tension in her face and her
slow breathing that she wasn't faking, and it gave
him an opportunity to look his fill at her. He slid
beneath the covers to lie on his side, propping his
jaw on a fist as he studied her face.

How long would she go along with this? After
years of being solely under Sondra's influence,
Lainey might have learned to be adept at imitating
her mother's two-faced shenanigans. It was plain
Lainey was wary of him, that she didn't truly want
to live up to her vows.

Gabe reached over to gently pluck a strand of hair
that lay on Lainey's flushed cheek to pull it aside
and tuck it in with the rest of her hair. The silky
texture made the strand difficult to release, so he
took a moment to savor the feel of it as he rolled it
softly between his thumb and finger.

He tenderly laid the strand aside, then couldn't
resist brushing the back of a knuckle against her
flawless cheek. Five years of anger and frustration
had perpetually nettled him and tonight was no dif-

ferent. Except it was suddenly stronger because he was lying next to the cause.

Though Lainey claimed to have wised up and seemed to be suffering guilt, it'd take a fair amount of will and determination to redeem herself. If she wanted to. Besides, even he wouldn't risk raising babies with a woman who couldn't keep her word.

That's why he aimed to push her. These next days—weeks if she stuck it out—would give them both plenty of opportunities to see if she was as serious about making good on her vows as he was with his. And if she could be trusted.

Gabe rolled away then and switched off the light before he settled on his back and drew the covers up. He laid in the dark a long time, hearing every breath Lainey took. He didn't let himself think about the outcome he'd waited years for, because he'd waited for it too long to completely believe it could truly happen now. With Lainey.

And he couldn't let himself think about the way she'd felt in his arms. Particularly since his insistence that she share his bed was suddenly a far more rigorous test of his self-control than it was a test of her sincerity.

No alarm clock had gone off, but something had roused her. Lainey rolled from her stomach to her right side before she realized that the mattress by her hip was oddly slanted. She opened her eyes and jerked with surprise before she rose up on an elbow.

The light from the master bath softly illuminated the big bedroom enough for her to see that Gabe sat on the bed beside her, dressed for a day of hard work. She belatedly reached for the edge of the covers to pull them higher as he spoke, his voice still rusty from sleep.

"Figured you'd have trouble getting used to the earlier hours we keep out here."

With that, he handed her a mug of steaming black coffee. Only then did her drowsy sense of smell detect the rich aroma, and she automatically tried to take the mug. The fact that Gabe held on to it until he was certain she had it in a steady grip meant that for several moments her fingers were closed over his. Her heart fluttered from the tingling sensation of her small fingers curled around his large, hard ones.

While he still had a good grip on her coffee, she slid up higher in the bed so she could take the mug in both hands. Gabe waited until she did then released it completely to her.

"What time is it?" she croaked before she took a bracing sip of the bitter brew.

"Just before five."

Lainey only barely suppressed a groan. She hadn't seen this side of five a.m. since she'd left

Texas, and though she'd slept surprisingly well, she hadn't given a thought to how early Gabe might have expected her to get up.

"I don't suppose there's any chance I could stay in bed until seven or so?" she asked, then had another sip of coffee.

"Too soft and citified to keep up?"

Lainey studied the rugged planes of his face. Gabe's expression was as tough as ever, but an appealing gleam of humor showed briefly in his dark eyes.

"You think I can't keep up with a real he-man?"

Gabe's stern mouth curved faintly in as much of a smile as she'd seen so far. "Maybe in a few days you'll be able to sit a horse for more than a couple hours. Probably take a good six weeks to get close to a real day's work."

Lainey sipped her coffee again, recognizing this for what it was. It was not a dare, but a few moments of gentle teasing. She'd indulged in that same kind of thing with town friends who'd come out to her father's ranch. Since she'd long since gone soft and become citified, she was fair game and they both knew it.

"Six whole weeks, huh?"

"We keep a lace pillow in the mudroom for city slickers."

Lainey rolled her eyes, unable to keep a wry smile

off her face. She was savvy enough about ranch work to know she couldn't just stroll back into it at the level she'd left it, but that didn't mean it wouldn't all come back to her.

"All right, Mr. Macho. Just don't give me a bronc the first day out."

"Oh, no, ma'am."

Now Gabe did smile at her. An actual smile that creased his lean cheeks and transformed him into the handsomest man she'd ever seen. The sudden closeness she felt toward him took her by surprise and she felt warmth radiate through her.

It was then that Lainey realized how little self-consciousness she felt lying in Gabe's bed talking to him while he sat next to her on its edge. She'd never known when he'd come to bed or when he'd gotten up. He'd done nothing to disturb her the entire night, so perhaps part of her ease now was because she felt a level of trust toward him.

And this small bit of gentle teasing made her feel connected to him, as if some fragile tendril of companionship was beginning to grow.

For the first time in weeks, Lainey felt almost lighthearted and more than a little optimistic. She had the sense that some boundary between them had fallen, though she couldn't have said precisely what it was, only that she suddenly felt better than she'd felt in a long time.

Until Gabe's smile eased into its usual stern line and took the spark of humor and feeling of closeness with it.

"I'll see you at breakfast."

He stood then and picked up his half-empty mug from where it sat on the night table next to hers before he strode out of the room and pulled the door to the hall closed.

It was as if he'd relaxed a few moments then caught himself mellowing toward her and put an abrupt stop to it. Like the kiss last night. One moment he was as caught up in the sensuality and closeness of it as she was, the next he was stone-faced again and closed off.

But why wouldn't he be? He didn't trust her at all, and everything between them was precarious. It was a harsh reminder that Lainey had a lot to make up for, a lot to prove. So much that it might be impossible to do.

Lainey got out of bed then went to the closet to grab what few work-sturdy clothes she'd brought with her.

CHAPTER FIVE

BREAKFAST was largely silent, and Lainey's earlier optimism faded even more. Judging from the way things were going now, those moments of ease between them earlier might never have happened.

Gabe scanned a part of the newspaper as he ate. His one-word responses to a couple of her comments and the fact that he didn't initiate conversation made her even more aware of the renewed distance between them.

Because it was a long time until the noon meal, Lainey packed away a full breakfast. It was the most she'd been able to eat at a meal for weeks, so at least that was an improvement. Lainey remembered well how much energy good food could generate, and she'd need it for ranch work. Even being outdoors in the fresh air would be tiring until she adjusted, so she wanted to do whatever she could to minimize it.

In spite of her mother's loud and continual objections when she'd been growing up, Lainey's father had raised her to work as hard as he would have a son, to acquire as much skill and stamina as any man. She probably hadn't lost the knack or weakened to uselessness, but her challenge these next days would be to prevent her enthusiasm from overwhelming her common sense.

What helped make up for her disappointment now was the excitement she felt at the thought of being on a horse again. It still amazed her that she'd stayed away from Texas so long. She hadn't bothered going to riding stables in and near Chicago for an occasional ride because her mother's demands had severely curtailed her free time. The limits of a bridle path or little real access to vast spaces had made the notion less appealing.

Even a job had been difficult to pursue because Sondra's troubles and constant ailments made it difficult for Lainey to both find a job she liked and to be dependable once she was hired. Because finding substitute help had been eternally frustrating— mostly because her mother was so rude to them— Lainey had eventually given up on the idea of a job.

Sondra's problems had been frustrating to deal with. Despite Lainey's objections, Sondra had chosen doctors who seemed more inclined to take orders from her rather than stand behind the need for specific tests to form their own diagnoses and treatment recommendations.

Then last year, Sondra had gone into a steady emotional decline, until her sudden death in a car accident just after the first of the year had ended it all.

Lainey still wondered if her mother's troubles had been rooted in bitterness and guilt, or if they'd been the result of some sort of mental illness that had impaired her judgment. Since Sondra had scorned counseling of any kind, Lainey figured she'd never know.

After the wreck, Lainey had begun to start the search for a job, but working day in and day out in a climate-controlled building had surprisingly little appeal. She'd actually thought more than once about swallowing her pride and coming home to live on Talbot. But by then she'd started to go through her mother's personal papers and had rapidly concluded that making plans to return to Texas—at least for a while—was unavoidable.

And now Gabe expected her to stay and finally live up to her vows. If things went well between them, the bonus would be that she'd finally get to live the kind of life she'd missed and preferred to anything else.

In the meantime, whatever happened with Gabe, she'd enjoy living on a ranch again. And since some of the most challenging and rewarding aspects of ranching had to do with horses, she was eager to get down to the stable and choose a mount.

Gabe finally set aside the paper. He'd silently of-

fered it to her earlier, but she'd declined, too focused
on her thoughts to concentrate on the news or mar-
kets. When he glanced her way and saw she was
finished eating, he started to rise. She did too before
he could make the gentlemanly gesture of pulling
out her chair.

"I need to put my hair up," she told him then
went to the small bathroom just off the hall from
the kitchen.

After quickly tying her hair up, she generously
applied sunblock and slid the tube into her back
jeans pocket. Lainey wasn't certain what to expect
that morning except that she didn't want to slow
Gabe down any more than necessary. She got her
hat and joined him on the back patio for the walk
to the barns.

Instead of starting out on horseback, they took
Gabe's pickup for a long tour of several of the stock
tanks and windmills farthest from the headquarters.
They stopped to tinker with a couple, checked one
of the metal tanks for a leak that had been repaired
the week before, then came back to the stable at
midmorning.

Lainey was uneasy with the ongoing silence between them. Gabe had only spoken when absolutely
necessary, and nothing he'd said had been remotely
personal. She was wondering whether to initiate
conversation when they got back to the stable at the

headquarters, but Gabe seemed to loosen up once they were inside.

"The calmest horse I've got with the smoothest gait is that little sorrel in the fourth stall." Now he glanced her way. "You can chose any horse you want, but that'd be my pick until you get used to riding again."

They'd stopped in front of the stall where Gabe's black gelding was. He reached for a bridle and opened the stall gate.

"If you want to saddle her yourself, the one on the hay bale by her stall'll do."

The black gelding stepped forward and Gabe efficiently put the bridle on the horse before he led him out. Lainey walked on to the sorrel's stall and opened the gate to take a few moments to get acquainted with the pretty mare before she slipped the bridle on then led her out for a quick grooming.

The familiar tasks were satisfying, and when she was finished, she took another moment to pet the mare. As Gabe led his gelding past, Lainey started after him with the mare and fell into step beside him.

"You didn't mention her name," Lainey said, eager to get him to talk.

He glanced her way briefly before he faced forward. "You one who needs to know names first?"

"You don't?"

"Doll," he said gruffly, and Lainey got the impression that the name wasn't one he was comfortable telling her. His dark eyes shifted back to hers, as if he knew what she'd ask next. "As in, 'She's a doll.' Sweet-tempered, gracious."

"Did you name her that?"

"She's got a registered name. Someone referred to her that way, and it stuck."

"Ah."

Now she saw the faint twinkle show in his dark eyes and smiled. "Was that someone you?"

He looked away from her again. "It's not seemly to ask a man if he's got a little whimsy in his soul," he said as they neared the far doors. His profile was stern again, but she suddenly sensed that there might be a fair amount of whimsy in Gabriel Patton. It fit the softness she sometimes got a glimpse of.

"What about your black? What do you call him?"

"Duke when he acts it. Knothead when he doesn't."

Lainey smiled, not surprised. "Wouldn't do for the boss to ride a horse with a wimpy name."

"See you remember that." Now he slanted her a mock-stern glance.

"Who usually rides Doll?"

"Kids and city folk. Usually worked by one of the men to keep her active…how come you're so inquisitive?"

Lainey came right back with, "You haven't been much for conversation this morning. Since I thought we were going to get to know each other..." She let her sentence fade.

"Lots of ways to get to know someone."

The subject was closing again—he was closing off again—and she didn't want to allow it.

"I thought this would be a crash course."

They stepped out in the sun and Gabe turned to check his cinch. He gathered the reins, then mounted. "Folks can fool you with talk. Actions speak truer."

"Do you mean me?" she asked, still on the ground looking up at him.

"That's an observation of human nature."

Her spirits sank a little. "I don't think so. You mean me."

Gabe leaned forward a bit to rest a forearm on the saddle horn and looked down at her. "That's the other hazard," he said bluntly. "Too much talk, and things are bound to get said that aren't meant."

"When that happens, there should be more talk until both parties are clear."

His gaze sharpened to probe hers. "You're eager to prove yourself. Or convince me of something."

That was certainly true, but she couldn't tell whether he understood that or not, or whether he approved. And she couldn't have missed the message that he was far from trusting her.

"If you'd done what I have, what would you want to do?"

His gaze shifted away as he straightened and switched the reins to his right hand. He wasn't going to answer and it frustrated her, so she pressed on quietly.

"There've been too many hard feelings between us to avoid talking about them now. Or just talking, getting to know each other."

His gaze came back down to hers. "That's true, Mrs. Patton, but just now we need to concentrate on checking a herd that needs to be moved before noon." He nodded toward the mare. "If you're going along, best mount up."

With that the black stepped forward, clearly impatient because Gabe held him to a walk to give her a few moments to catch up. Stung by this new taste of implacability, Lainey watched him go then turned to the mare. A hefty measure of the pleasure of finally being able to ride that morning had dimmed.

The rest of the day was as silent between them as the morning had been. Lainey knew Gabe was a laconic man, but as the afternoon went on, his silence felt more and more like retribution. She could hardly blame him.

Because she'd turned into a bitter, vengeful shrew who'd done spiteful things to get back at him, she couldn't expect Gabe to easily set aside what she'd done to him or be able to easily resist the temptation of doing to her what she'd done to him.

Because he'd been so silent today, she'd been unable to keep from mentally reliving the five years of silence she'd inflicted on him. She'd had most of the day to remember the times she'd rebuffed the requests for contact that he'd sent to her lawyer. She'd never forget each and every letter and package he'd mailed at holidays or on her birthdays, along with a handful of others sent at other times that she'd refused to open.

There were so many things she wished she could do over or somehow erase from everyone's memory. Once or twice might not have been so bad, but she'd done it repeatedly for almost five whole years. It jolted her to think about how long five years was, and how long she'd been so hateful. She'd lived those years in a kind of delusion, and shuddered to think about how much longer she might have gone on had her mother not died. Her confidence in her judgment had been shaken from top to bottom, and Lainey felt incapable of making the right choices now. Particularly about the marriage Gabe expected of her.

For as long as she lived she'd never say or do, or

even think, spitefully about anyone for any reason. The vengeful temper and self-righteous pride she'd been so filled with had been brutally crushed. The guilt she felt about it all had been burning inside her for weeks now and still it burned.

They drove back to the house just before supper. After moving cattle that morning, they'd spent the rest of the day going from task to task on the ranch, using the pickup most of the time. Lainey suspected Gabe was trying to minimize her time on horseback because she wasn't used to it, though his preference might have been to be in the saddle the whole day.

And he'd kept her out of the heat for long stretches. Though Lainey hadn't complained, Gabe seemed to know it bothered her. She doubted very much that in the normal course of his day Gabe would have kept the pickup's air-conditioning on high. In fact, she remembered he'd often driven his cars and his pickups with the windows down because he loved being outdoors.

Elisa had the meal on the table when they came in, which was an hour earlier than last night. Gabe might be in the habit of showering before he'd sat down to the evening meal so since they only took time to wash up, it was clear he must have altered his routine to accommodate her.

After a day in the outdoors, Lainey was ravenous. She all but inhaled her food, drinking two big glasses of ice water before a full stomach and the cool house began to revive her a bit. Gabe insisted she shower while he checked messages, so Lainey grabbed a set of clean clothes and shut herself in the bathroom.

The hot shower soothed most of her aches, and afterward she used a blow-dryer on her hair. She lightly applied aloe vera to the places on her face that had gone pink wherever she'd sweated or rubbed off her sunblock, before she put on a bit of makeup. Lainey had just dressed in the denim skirt and blue blouse she'd brought in with her and stepped out of the bathroom, when Gabe walked in from the hall.

She'd decided to go barefoot the rest of the evening, but when she saw the faint gleam that came into Gabe's gaze as it slid down the front of her and fixed on her bare feet, she felt self-conscious about the choice.

His gruff, "Very pretty feet, Mrs. Patton," was the last comment she expected. But then his gaze came slowly back up, lingering faintly here and there to set off small flashes of heat before it connected with hers.

"Thank you," she said softly.

"Elisa's got coffee in the den, if you want some."

Lainey nodded, hoping for something more, but Gabe strode on to the big closet. She watched him all the way there, disrupted by another small hit-and-run conversation. And his use of the words *Mrs. Patton.* No one looking at the two of them or listening to a stray bit of what they'd said to each other that day, would have been able to identify her as Mrs. Patton.

The nettle of hurt she felt about that surprised her. She hadn't thought of herself at all in terms of being Mrs. Patton, but it stunned her to realize that not only had her thinking changed, but that she might actually want to *be* Mrs. Patton.

Gabe had addressed her that way as if it was a long-standing truth for him. He'd already made clear that he expected everything of her that the title represented. And yet once he'd kissed her last night, he'd treated her with little more familiarly than he might a houseguest he was considerate of but wasn't too interested in.

The fact that he was again leaving the closet door open while he pried off his boots on the bootjack and methodically undressed seemed significant somehow, though he might as well have been standing in the next county.

He'd gone from putting her on the spot with that kiss last night to abruptly walking away, undressing with the door open as if it was normal for there to be no closed doors between them. And yet he'd locked away any bit of feeling between them and made it seem as if the kiss had never happened.

Gabe peeled his shirt off and tossed it into the bin set apart for laundry, then started on his belt buckle. Lainey's gaze shifted away and she walked quietly toward the hall door.

By the time she got to the den, poured a cup of coffee and chose a place to sit on the leather sofa, she began to think about things from Gabe's perspective.

Perhaps he'd taken seriously her remark about waiting for genuine feeling between them, and was now determined to do nothing to push her into a show of affection. It made Lainey feel tender toward him to think that. The fact that he'd kept a respectful physical distance from her seemed to confirm her conclusion.

Gabe didn't have to verbally navigate boardroom politics and offices full of people who chatted through the day or wrote and read memos or shuffled papers or communicated via computer screens. It wasn't that Gabe couldn't verbally navigate boardrooms or offices, because a large portion of his success had come from doing just that. It was just more natural for him to work with laconic men of action like himself and animals that didn't speak. He'd long ago learned to watch for signs and signals to make his determinations and come to sound decisions.

Actions speak truer.

Lainey strongly doubted he'd continue in a marriage or have children with a woman who wasn't as honorable as he was. So of course everything she said would be weighed against her actions.

Even she knew it was possible for an apology to be nothing more than an insincere token of politeness, self-serving rather than heartfelt or worse, a selfish manipulation. The proof of a fully sincere apology depended on the later actions of the person who'd made the apology. Did their behavior change? Did they demonstrate by their behavior a determination never to give the offense again?

Lainey sipped her coffee and let her gaze scan the room, shifting from one small sculpture or artifact to another on the many shelves in the bookcases around her as she mulled it over. She was so absorbed by her thoughts that she didn't hear Gabe's bootsteps in the hall. When he stepped into the room, she glanced toward the open door.

The instant her gaze made contact with the waiting look in Gabe's, she realized his dark gaze must have fixed on her the moment she was in sight. Something flickered in his eyes before his gaze shifted and he crossed the room to his desk.

CHAPTER SIX

GABE was dressed in a white shirt and jeans, but different boots than he'd worn outside today. The white shirt set off his tan and gave his dark eyes a soft brightness that drew her to watch them.

Lainey sensed the faint tension about him. Not anger. Maybe energy, but certainly in keeping with his natural intensity. Lainey felt her body begin to react to whatever it was she sensed in him and felt a tingle of feminine excitement.

His dark gaze came up from scanning some papers on the top of the desk to meet hers. "Do you want to have a look at an overview of Talbot's records?"

Lainey eased forward on the sofa. "Sure. Would you like coffee?"

"Thanks."

She reached to pour his cup and refill hers from the insulated carafe on the coffee table. Assuming the overview would be on the computer, she was about to stand when Gabe noticed.

"It's a printout, so stay where you are." Gabe picked up a set of pages and came around the desk to the sofa. He sat down beside her and took the cup she offered as he passed her the printed sheets.

Lainey paused to have another sip of coffee before she set her cup down to ease back on the sofa. Because the sofa was leather and Gabe outweighed her, she slid closer to him than she'd meant to, so her hip and thigh settled lightly against his. Her impulse was to move away, but she was wary of offending him. Lainey stayed where she was and casually leaned back as she would have if she'd not ended up so close to him. She couldn't help it that her arm wedged against his.

The furnace-like heat of Gabe's big body radiated along her side from shoulder to thigh, causing the listings and figures she slowly paged through to read like gibberish. She felt the subtle tension in Gabe seep into her.

Mental pictures of the various ploys her adolescent dates had used to engineer accidental touches—that were anything but accidental—played through her mind. Though she hadn't done it on purpose, maybe Gabe would accept it as some signal of interest, if he interpreted it that way.

If he still wanted this marriage they'd have to do something to close the distance between them soon. If he'd already changed his mind about staying married to her, she needed to know before they slept together another night. Nervousness almost made her chicken out before she could think of a way to open the subject.

Knowing it was only a matter of seconds before he'd realize she wasn't really reading the pages, Lainey forced herself to look at him.

"Could I look at these tomorrow when my mind is a little sharper?" She didn't realize when she handed him the papers that her hand was trembling until she looked away from the probe of his gaze and caught sight of the faint flutter.

Gabe took the pages to set them and his nearly empty cup on the side table next to him, but he didn't remark. Lainey hesitated to look completely away from him, so she was still staring where the trembling pages had been. She raced to think of something to say.

If he'd already changed his mind, it could also account for his near silence and persistent remoteness. It was amazing how difficult it was to speak the actual words that would lead up to a straightforward question.

"You said last night that I might feel more at ease if I did some of the things a wife might do." Lainey cringed inwardly at the artless opening, but she dared to look at him and forced herself to go on.

"The outcome went well, or it seemed to, but I can't help noticing that you didn't...well, there's been no sign you found it…thought of it…like I did, so…''

Lainey knew right away that not only had her daring exceeded her courage but that she'd turned into a babbling idiot. The sharpness in his gaze had disrupted her ability to hold her train of thought. She suddenly wished she'd just read the papers and kept silent.

''So?'' he prompted, and his dark eyes began to glitter. Lainey felt the tension in his big body grow more taut, though he looked completely at ease. There was no hint of anger in him, nothing to warn her that she was treading on thin ice. She tried to sound more coherent as she got to the question she'd meant to ask.

''So, since the last thing I heard from you on the subject is that you want me to live up to my vows, I wondered if you had reconsidered since then, or if you were…waiting.'' She had to pause to try to swallow away the dryness in her throat. ''On me. I mean—waiting on me. Or maybe waiting on the…situation.''

''Which do you think it is?''

He'd asked in a low, no-nonsense tone, and she searched his gaze, trying to discern the answer before she could hazard a guess—or to at least detect some sign that bringing this subject up was safe to do. She could tell he might be interested in what she'd say, but only marginally.

The thought that she might have stumbled onto a conversation he wouldn't cut short encouraged her to blunder on and risk a guess.

"Maybe it's a combination of those things. You maybe have doubts about whether you can trust me enough to stay married, but you're also waiting for the situation to…improve. Either way, you're waiting for something, probably looking for something to show in me. S-something that will redeem my past behavior. Or maybe waiting for me to…do something."

Lainey felt her face go hot. She was mangling it, probably missing the right answer by a mile, even if he could make sense of what she'd said. *She* wasn't sure she could make sense of what she'd just said!

The whole time Gabe had sat there, his gaze calmly probing hers then shifting to search her face as she'd become more flustered. But he'd given no clue that she'd either guessed right or that he'd tell her so even if she had.

Because he was a man who judged situations by observation as much as words, Gabe was quite good at concealing his own thoughts. There wasn't a hint of what he might be thinking, which made her believe she'd missed on every count. If so, she couldn't imagine the reason for his distance, unless he just plain loathed her.

And yet he hadn't closed the subject or cut her off, so she wondered why the silence stretched. Lainey had to look away from the laser search he made of her face. Frustration made it difficult to keep from giving up completely.

She'd been here little more than twenty-four hours, but she wasn't sure she could continue like this. She certainly couldn't consider intimacy with Gabe, much less have his children unless something radically changed. Though it couldn't have been more than ten seconds since she'd finished speaking, Lainey was suddenly impatient.

"You're right about too much talk. Things do get said, lots of them not very clear or coherent." She started to slide to the edge of the sofa and stand, but Gabe caught her wrist to stop her and her gaze flew to his.

His expression was stony, but his eyes held a fiery darkness. The showery tingles that radiated from his light grip caused a peculiar weakness to follow in their wake.

"I'm waiting for you Lainey," he drawled before his voice went grim. "Waiting to see if all you really came here for was to humor me. You know I can petition the courts to compensate my investment in Talbot, and I'd probably win. Maybe you're thinking if you played everything just so, wrapped me around your little finger, maybe you'd get me to promise to let it go back to you. Intact.''

Lainey stared at his implacable expression, stunned. This explained a lot. A huge knot of misery rose into her throat and pounded sickly. She couldn't get the words past it at first and when she could, her voice was hoarse.

''I deserve that,'' she admitted quietly.

Though she'd more than earned his mistrust, she couldn't help the craving to somehow defend herself, since the only real defense she had in any part of what she'd done was on the subject of Talbot Ranch.

''I spoke to my lawyer about compensation for Talbot before I left Chicago. I'll call him tomorrow and tell him to get started. Your attorney will probably get a call soon, so you might want to make sure he's prepared.''

Lainey started to pull her wrist from his light grip but his fingers flexed to keep her there. He wasn't finished with her, but she already knew what he'd say next. If she was right, then she might as well say it first.

''Would you rather I just pack my bags?''

''Leave the bags where they are.''

The growling sound of that sent a shiver of wariness through her.

"What's the point? You'll be getting the major portion of Talbot whatever happens between you and me." She tried again to pull her wrist from Gabe's grip, but it was immovable.

His dark eyes began to glitter. Lainey was suddenly desperate to get him to see sense. They had absolutely no foundation for marriage but a piece of paper and vows neither of them could honestly live up to at this late date.

"I think we both know going on with this marriage will only prevent you from finding someone you could truly be happy with."

"You don't want to mix a mongrel with the Talbot pedigree."

The out-of-the-blue remark completely stunned her, and Lainey searched his dark eyes. The hardness she saw there told her he was completely serious. She knew instinctively this was no spur of the moment notion, but some long-standing belief. She'd never given a thought to the fact that Gabe's impoverished upbringing might have caused him think of himself as less than anyone. Particularly after the success he'd proved himself to be.

Now she remembered the rumors of the women who'd pursued him while he was still a work-for-wages cowhand. Had some of them given him that impression, or worse, said so? Whatever the cause for his belief, it was absolutely shocking to realize he'd as much as confessed it to her.

"No, that's not true—it was never true," she said hastily, so anxious to correct his impression and to demonstrate her sincerity that she put her free hand over the one that gripped her wrist. She didn't pay attention to her next words before they were out. "I loved you once."

It was as if her urgent declaration had set off a giant boom of thunder in the room. The glitter in Gabe's eyes suddenly burst into a dark conflagration and she went light-headed with alarm.

Oh, God, had she made him angry? Did he think she was lying?

The chances of that were greater than of him believing her so long after the fact. Years ago, she'd thought her only protection from the humiliation of being rejected was to keep her feelings for Gabe hidden. To reveal them at this late date, even though she didn't still love him, would either make her look like a liar now or a liar back then. Even if Gabe believed her, the danger was that he would use the unintended confession to hurt and humiliate her.

"Do it." His terse order wasn't what she'd expected.

"Do...what?"

"Call your lawyer tomorrow. Early."

Shocked by the abrupt demand, Lainey gave a

small nod. Was he ignoring what she'd said about loving him once? Did that mean he thought she was lying and he'd take her offer of compensation then order her to leave?

Lainey started to take her hand off his and pull away, but he caught it to tug her close. She suddenly knew what would happen now, she could see it in his eyes, though she couldn't understand why. She'd no more than registered the impression when his arm came tightly around her and he slipped his other hand to her head to force her soft lips against his.

This wasn't the tender, expertly sensual kiss of last night. It was devouring and carnal, like a conqueror ruthlessly seizing the delicate spoils of a vanquished enemy and taking a lusty bite. And yet there was no brutality in his kiss, just an all-consuming sexual rawness that staggered her brain and immediately turned her into a weakling who could do no more than cling to him and shakily submit.

Whatever his kiss had been last night, it hadn't taken over her will like this one did. Suddenly she wasn't only clinging to him, she was on his lap, shoving her fingers into his long hair and making fists to hang on. Her own feminine drive shocked her as he masterfully drove it to the surface until she was meeting him kiss for kiss, pressing herself restlessly into him, desperate for more.

She was on fire, wildly on fire, and she was too

dizzy from the roaring heat to realize the desperate little sounds she dimly heard were her own or that her body was all but shouting that she was his for the taking.

To have Gabe wrench his mouth from hers without warning as he called out a gruff, "Who the hell is it?" made her jerk and reflexively pull back. His hard arms kept her tightly against him, and she realized he was calling out to someone, probably Elisa.

Belatedly she remembered that the door to the hall was open, and she glanced dazedly toward it. Now she heard Elisa's voice from down the hall in the direction of the living room, though she was nowhere in sight.

"Señorita McClain to see you, Señor Gabe."

"Tell her we'll be right out."

Lainey's neck didn't seem strong enough to support her head and she dropped her forehead to his hard shoulder. She was still panting in the aftermath of that devastating kiss, and her skin felt as if it had been sensitized with sandpaper. Every feminine place inside her was still heavy and heated, and for the first time in her life, Lainey felt the barbed wire nettles of frustrated desire.

"If you don't get up, I'll never cool off enough for company," he growled, his hot breath gusting into her hair.

His voice was harsh, but his hands still moved on her as if he couldn't get enough. Lainey lifted her head, unable to look him in the eye, and tried to compose herself. She realized from the cool air that hit her that her blouse had come unbuttoned and had pulled from the waistband of her denim skirt. She could tell by putting up a hand that her hair was a mess because Gabe's fingers had clutched and combed through it as eagerly as her fingers had his.

Somehow she managed to move off his lap and stand on legs that still felt heavy and weak. Gabe got up, but she couldn't look at him. He caught her hand and led her to the French doors behind his desk. Lainey gripped the gap of her blouse closed as they stepped out on the patio then walked to the master bedroom. Gabe let her go in ahead of him.

"Best straighten yourself before you come out."

Lainey glanced at him as he strode to the dresser to run a flat brush through his hair before he walked to the hall door to leave, efficiently smoothing a couple loosened riffles of his shirt into the belted waist of his jeans as he did. He didn't spare her a single glance the whole way.

Still shaky, but rapidly returning to her senses, Lainey straightened her clothes and brushed her hair before she took an extra few moments to splash her face with cold water. A last look in the big mirror in the bathroom told her she still looked flushed and dazed, and from the slight swell of her soft lips, she'd obviously just been kissed to within an inch of her life.

She found her sandals and walked into the hall.

Señorita McClain, Elisa had said. *Cassidy McClain*—Cassie—one of the last people Lainey would want to face after that kiss. Cassie had been the high school nemesis who'd constantly competed with her in everything, from ranching to grades to sports to boys.

Lainey had been popular enough in school, but not nearly as popular as blond-haired, blue-eyed Cassie McClain. No one had been. But while Cassie was bold and outgoing, Lainey had been quieter and more reserved, struggling to behave like a lady, gracious in defeat even if it killed her, but also modest in her few victories over the very competitive Cassie.

At least the discomfort of facing Cassie again when she, as well as everyone else in a four-county area, knew what Lainey had done to Gabe, would distract her from the worry of the other thoughts that were just beginning to dawn on her passion-dazed brain. The ones about the weapon she'd just handed Gabe.

And her own weak-willed participation in whatever he might secretly have in mind to humiliate her.

*   *   *

Many girls had a nemesis of some kind in high school. It was usually someone popular and gorgeous and clever, a nemesis who had the social clout to make them feel inadequate and awful, and who might not hesitate to use it.

When Lainey found the courage to face Cassie again, she pasted a calm smile on her face and walked into the big living room as Cassie sat down on the sofa. She arrived just in time to see Gabe hand Cassie a tumbler of iced tea. Cassie batted her big blue eyes up at him and smiled with appealing sweetness.

But it wasn't Cassie's face Lainey paid attention to, it was Gabe's. He was actually smiling in a way that creased his lean cheeks and made him look not only devastatingly handsome but wholly approachable. And he bestowed that smile on Cassie so effortlessly that Lainey couldn't help but feel miserable. She would have had trouble even looking at another man after that kiss, much less be able to smile like Gabe was with any sort of ease or enthusiasm.

Lainey was certain neither of them had noticed her arrival until Gabe said, "Here's Lainey now," as he moved toward the overstuffed chair next to the end of the sofa where Cassie had chosen to sit.

Cassie glanced her way just as Lainey reached them and smiled, but Lainey noticed her smile had a sly curl on one side that Gabe wouldn't be able to see from his view of Cassie's profile. Lainey tensed for the opening salvo.

"Long time, no see, Lainey. Is this just a quick visit or are you here to stay?"

One of the most annoying things about Cassie was that she could unerringly target Lainey's most uncomfortable subjects, and she'd never been shy about bluntly bringing them up. Since this wasn't a question Lainey dared answer either way, she decided to meet Cassie's provocative question with one of her own. Two could play at this game, and Lainey tried for a convincing smile as she chose a seat on an overstuffed chair across from the sofa. Gabe waited to sit down until after she did.

"I was about to ask you the same question, Cass," Lainey said, then quickly injected false enthusiasm into her voice as she added, "How *are* you?"

She saw the faint surprise in Cassie's eyes, but tried not to notice that Gabe's big fingers drummed once on the arm of his chair. Because she didn't look, she had no idea if it was a reaction to her comeback to Cassie or not, though there was no way it couldn't be.

The surprise in Cassie's eyes shifted to a look of orneriness and she gave a dismissive wave of her hand.

"Just out drivin' around. Thought I'd remind Gabe of Daddy's barbecue Saturday night and see if I could coax him to come. It seems like *years* since Gabe's gotten out to socialize."

Lainey smiled, but realized grimly that their not-quite-polite banter could rapidly escalate. Though she'd tried to ignore Cassie's occasional barbs in high school and had allowed most without giving a comeback, she was too sensitive about what she'd done to Gabe to either ignore or allow them now.

"Has he given you an answer yet?"

As she asked the question, Lainey caught sight of the somber look Gabe gave her, but shifted her gaze back to Cassie.

"I hadn't got around to askin' him yet," Cassie replied, then allowed a meaningful pause before she added, "Of course, Daddy would consider it rude to mention it in front of you and leave you out, so you're invited, too."

There couldn't have been a better way to put it to send the message that Cassie had just stooped to toss her a bone. Lainey might have been shocked if she hadn't known what Cassie could be like, but she was surprised she'd keep it up in front of Gabe.

On the other hand, perhaps Cassie had designs on Gabe. Back in school, a method Cassie had used at least once when she'd zeroed in on a potential boyfriend had been to subtly expose the flaws or short-comings of the girl he was seeing at the time.

Public embarrassment was a handy weapon, and since Lainey was vulnerable to it on a grand scale these days, she might be in for torture anywhere she showed up that Cassie was present.

Lainey had just formulated a dandy comeback when she suddenly realized what she was about to do. Though it was difficult to keep the comeback to herself, she had to. Not just because Gabe was listening to every word, but because she'd promised herself. She gave Cassie as gracious a smile as she could manage.

"Why thank you, Cassie," she said, still straining a bit as she realized how difficult it was to just lay down and take it. But since it hadn't killed her to go this far, Lainey added a more enthusiastic, "Your daddy always threw great barbecues. Is he still using his special recipe?"

Mac McClain's special barbecue recipe was truly noteworthy, and it was a compliment to bring it up. And bringing it up now was a signal to Gabe that Lainey had traded all the barbs she was going to with Cassie McClain. She was not as brash and daring as Cassie, particularly in front of Gabe, but he might already take a dim view of the way she'd started to treat a guest in his home. Besides which, she was the true outsider here, not Cassie.

"Oh, my stars, yes! It's been so long I didn't think you'd remember Daddy's special recipe."

Clearly Cassie wasn't going to back off, so Lainey kept her benign smile in place and tried to be pleasant. "How is your daddy?"

Cassie gave a frivolous wave of her hand. "He's five years older since you saw him last, but you'd never know it, handsome old devil that he is. He's still got enough vinegar to flirt with the women and outride the men."

The silence that descended then made Lainey even more aware that the source of that silence—and the place where most of the tension in the room had concentrated—was Gabe. There was a clear warning for her in what she sensed from him, so she didn't dare look his way. Obviously he expected her to respond in kind and he opposed it.

But instead of striking back, Lainey's gaze remained fixed on Cassie as she tried to find something mild but non-provoking to say next. Cassie stared back, waiting. One blond brow went up, almost inviting Lainey to make a comeback.

And then the entire conversation made a lightning replay through Lainey's mind. She felt a bubble of nervous amusement surge up into the awful silence and she was suddenly helpless to keep it suppressed.

CHAPTER SEVEN

THE bubble of nervous amusement felt suspiciously like a giggle as Cassie's latest *five years* crack replayed in Lainey's mind. It seemed so relentlessly juvenile that she couldn't help but see how ridiculous it was. If not for the situation with Gabe that Lainey herself had created, the natural competitiveness between her and Cassie would have spurred the woman to find any number of other things to target.

The small gurgle of amusement that defeated her control slipped out despite the effort to keep it to herself.

Lainey covered it with a smiling, "Oh, Cassie, you're not a day different." Then she added an inspired, "At this rate, you're still going to be gorgeous and young when the rest of us have wrinkled and gone gray. You surely do take after your daddy."

Lainey resisted the urge to think about how few other ways she'd noticed Cass take after her daddy. Mac McClain was cowboy gallant in the manner of good-hearted ol' Texas boys who were blunt, fun loving, and indulgent with their women. Mac adored his spoiled daughter and was completely blind to her faults. Which made him a lot like her own daddy. Lainey might never have been a bosom pal of Cassie's but she'd always liked Mac, and she'd always been welcome in his home.

It was clear by the faint confusion that showed on Cassie's beautiful face that she wasn't certain how to take what Lainey had said. She probably suspected that her "you're not a day different" was some sort of nudge, but it was obvious the compliment and the prediction of one-upmanship in the aging department far outweighed whatever offense there might have been before it.

Cassie actually smiled at Lainey then and without the sly quirk, it looked disarmingly genuine. "You know, we might drive down to San Antonio to shop sometime, Lainey. Just let me know when you're free."

The suggestion took Lainey completely by surprise. Was there something she'd missed? And yet she couldn't read anything in Cassie's face now that even hinted she had an ulterior motive, or that she'd only said what she had because Gabe could hear. If this was an olive branch of some kind, it was probably something she should accept.

"That might be fun, Cass. Thanks for the invitation."

Cassie actually looked pleased, and Lainey realized that she suddenly felt better.

She'd sworn to herself that she'd never do or say or even think anything spiteful about anyone again, and yet her first impulse with Cassie had been to do just that. She'd made a belated reversal to overcome it, and the result was vastly more satisfying than it would have been if she'd kept tossing back veiled insults.

Even if Cassie leveled a few more barbs, perhaps the best way to deal with her was to be kind, to disarm her with an honest compliment of some sort. At the very least, there'd be no petty verbal wars and no guilt involved afterward.

Gabe had remained silent since he'd sat down, though Lainey had felt his constant disapproval. She'd also felt his gaze cutting over her face, and she hadn't dared to look his way. Even though the crisis had passed and she sensed his tension had lowered, she still didn't look his way to confirm it.

Cassie set her tea glass aside as if she was about to leave. "Well, I oughta get home. Daddy wanted me to go over his list for Tia before she goes to town tomorrow for the last of the food."

Cassie rose gracefully, and Gabe stood in a show of politeness. Lainey stood also, and was again surprised when Cassie's words to Gabe included them both.

"I hope y'all can make it Saturday. You could come around early and sit with the liar's club while

Daddy watches over the beef and—'' Cassie grinned over at her ''—Lainey and I could laze around the pool and catch up on gossip. Otherwise, we'll eat at six.''

Gabe's solemn, ''Wouldn't miss it,'' seemed to please Cassie. They both escorted her to the door, just like a married couple would to see off a guest. She and Gabe lingered to watch as Cassie walked out to her car and got in to drive off.

Lainey stepped back then and Gabe closed the door. He'd said nothing to her since he'd left her in the bedroom a half hour or more ago, and he'd just accepted the invitation to a barbeque he'd apparently not been planning to attend.

She was already regretting his acceptance. Because Mac always invited everyone, there'd be a huge crowd. The fact that Lainey doubted she had the courage to face everyone made her dread it more by the moment. It was even possible that word would get around that she'd be coming, so every gossip in this part of Texas was bound to show up.

Gabe's stern question yanked her out of her thoughts.

''What changed your mind?''

Lainey knew what he was talking about. She'd started out trading barbs with Cassie, then backed off and actually handled the situation in a way that brought about an unexpectedly peaceful ending. But when she looked at Gabe, she still saw a hint of disapproval.

"It just suddenly seemed ridiculous."

"So that's the end to it?"

Lainey realized then that Gabe didn't believe her. As if she were the cause of whatever conflict there'd been between her and Cassie. But how would he really know she hadn't been? And why would he believe her if she told him so? After his experience with her, what else could he think?

The only thing she could say to reassure him, even though it was the truth, was, "Yes. As far as it's up to me, it's the end. If you still expect me to live here as your wife, I doubt you want me to trade insults with anyone."

"I do and that's right," he said, his low voice carrying a solemn weight as he remarked on both parts of her statement.

He'd looked so tough as he'd said it. Lainey suddenly knew he'd allow no more talk from her from here on about whether they ought to stay married or not, and certainly no more suggestions from her about how slim the chances were that they might ever have a normal marriage.

Overwhelmed by the sheer force of will she felt in him, Lainey realized afresh that the fact that they might never love each other had little to do with the duty Gabe was determined for them both to live up to. Particularly her.

"I'm tired," she said quietly, as much from the day as she was from the wasted effort to get him to see sense. "I'd like to make it an early night, if you don't mind."

The moment the words were out, Lainey worried that he'd think it was some sort of invitation. After all, she'd gone wild over that kiss, so maybe he'd figure there was no reason to prolong the sexual drought he'd mentioned last night.

"I've got bookwork," he said, and Lainey relaxed.

Suddenly they were back to silence. As they walked together down the hall and separated as he turned off to go into the den, Lainey sensed even more strongly his mistrust.

Nothing had been solved with either that kiss or her promise to call her lawyer in the morning. And certainly nothing between them had been solved just now when she'd proved herself determined to get along peacefully with Cassie.

If Gabe truly wanted no more discussions about divorce, then there wasn't much left to do but resign herself to whatever future they'd have together. Surely there was nothing worse than the guilt and emotional agony she'd suffered these last months.

At least she'd have a real chance to do what she'd

come here to do. Perhaps she could make up for what she'd done to Gabe, and since marriage seemed to be the way he wanted it done, then staying married might also be the way to make him forget how badly she'd treated him.

She'd figure out how to be the best wife she could. Even if Gabe could never bring himself to love her as he might have if this had been a love match, then perhaps it was up to her to make whatever good feelings they had toward each other be enough.

That night when Gabe came to bed, there was no hint of ease between them, though he laid down beside her, switched off the light and quietly murmured a gravelly "'night."

Still sleepless, Lainey laid there listening to him breathe, feeling herself melt in the heat that radiated from his big body, though they didn't touch. Her skin fairly sizzled with the memory of that kiss, and it was impossible not to think about what might happen if he kissed her now.

After a while, Lainey began to relax and her thoughts drifted back to her decision to fulfill her vows to Gabe. She made herself remember that her father had rewritten his will to protect and provide for her. Gabe Patton had been his choice to ensure those things.

Her daddy had been her hero, the man who'd steadfastly parented her, the man who'd been her wise counselor, showing her by example what honor and good character was. He'd expected a lot of her, and she'd worked hard to live up to it all, never dreaming there'd come a time when she'd doubt him and choose a path more compatible with her mother's hateful example than the sterling one he'd set.

Surely she could rely on the wisdom of his choice for her, even now. Though she was long overdue to properly honor that choice, she'd do it now however difficult it might be. Even if her marriage to Gabe ultimately failed, it wouldn't be her daddy's fault or even Gabe's. The fault would be solely her own.

Lainey tried to think of ways to overcome the distance between her and Gabe. She considered easing her hand over to touch his, but the last thing she wanted was to hint that she was ready for the physical side of marriage. Eventually, she stopped trying to figure it out and dropped off to sleep.

As always, it was one thing to make up your mind to do something and find the courage to act, but quite another to figure out how to follow through.

That next morning Gabe was up before she was, but instead of sitting on the side of the bed while she tasted the coffee he'd brought, he'd set it on the nightstand and merely touched her shoulder to rouse her. He'd towered nearby until he was sure she was awake enough to see that he'd put her cup within reach.

Not even her raspy, "Thanks," as she sat up and he started to walk away, or her belated call as he reached the hall door, "I should be the one bringing you coffee in the morning," got much more than a gruff "No trouble" out of Gabe before he closed the door behind him.

Lainey sipped her coffee then got out of bed to take it with her to gather her clothes. She quickly did something with her hair, applied a light bit of makeup, then grabbed her sunblock to hurry out to breakfast.

Gabe had the newspaper open, and though he closed it to rise and politely seat her, he spared Lainey no more than a nod and a glance that barely touched her face before he sat down. She might have considered a wifely kiss on the cheek, but Gabe's manner discouraged that notion. He opened the paper again and she felt it increase the distance between them.

As Lainey glanced again at the open newspaper, she suddenly had a flash of memory from the years her parents had been together. On the few mornings her mother had gotten up in time to have breakfast with her husband and daughter, she'd never failed to read the newspaper through most of the meal. Neither Lainey nor her father had managed to coax Sondra from behind it to give more than an annoyed comment here and there.

Start as you mean to go. Perhaps that wasn't a bad idea. Because Elisa would soon bring in their food, Lainey made a daring start. "Is there a comics section?"

That earned her a quick glance. "Most do." The faint crankiness in that came mostly from a low voice that hadn't been used much that morning.

"Do they run Cathy?"

"Cathy."

It was a question that sounded like a distracted statement, but he turned back to the paper and paged through to the comics' page to scan it.

"Doesn't run in this one."

Lainey briefly considered asking Gabe to read aloud one of the others—anything to get him to speak to her—but decided against it.

"Thanks for checking," she said then lifted a hand to her folded napkin to toy with the rolled seam.

Elisa brought in their food then. Though Gabe acknowledged Elisa's arrival with a gruff thanks, he continued reading his paper as the housekeeper set out their food. Lainey offered a quiet thanks before Elisa went out, then unfolded her napkin to start.

When she'd smoothed it on her lap and picked up her fork to dig in, she paused to note that Gabe was still absorbed in his paper.

She took a shallow breath and dared a soft, "The newspaper will be the same temperature in five minutes, Gabe, but your steak and eggs won't."

Gabe's dark gaze swung to make contact with hers, but she glanced down at her plate. He efficiently refolded his paper and set it aside, then reached for his napkin.

"Thank you, Lainey."

The words were something only fractionally better than a low growl. Lainey didn't let herself look over at him for several moments and when she did, she saw no hint of irritation, so she tried something he'd surely consider safe conversation.

"Have you decided on our plans for today?"

"Always," he answered then brought his dark gaze up to hers. "We'll ride while it's cooler, then come back for your call before we head over to Talbot Ranch. If you need something new to wear Saturday, we'll drive into San Antonio. If we don't shop, we'll come home and find some work."

Pleased that this was more conversation than they'd had at any meal so far, Lainey began to hope for more and speared a slice of melon with her fork to move it to her plate. "I didn't bring much with me, so I probably do need to find something for

Saturday. I could use more work clothes, unless I've got some old ones that still fit at Talbot.''

"Are you on the pill?"

Lainey's gaze leaped up to his, completely taken by surprise. Her face went hot and it took her a moment to regain her composure. She'd wanted him to talk, but she hadn't expected this. "N-no."

"Good."

Gabe returned his attention to his food as Lainey tried to recover from that. Surely he didn't expect her to conceive a child right away? Things were far too precarious between them. Mindful of his remark last night about mixing a mongrel with the Talbot pedigree, she was leery of offending him, so she started carefully.

"Pregnancies often seem to include things like morning sickness, moody emotions—"

Lainey cut herself off as Gabe's gaze shot to hers. She finished with a lame, "And there could be special health considerations. Horseback riding...other things," she said, then dared quietly, "It might be good to wait until things are more settled between us before we get to that stage. Which was why I'd thought about starting on the pill right away."

Lainey held her breath. Surely Gabe would understand that.

"Call Blake this morning."

The order to call one of the well-known local doctors was decisive, but she saw no sign that Gabe either resented her decision about going on the pill or had taken offense. "Then you don't object?"

The faint lift of his dark brows and the softening of his stern mouth suggested a touch of male horror. "Not after a list like that."

Lainey relaxed and smiled gently at him. "Thank you."

"Why thank me?"

"It was considerate, and I appreciate that. I've not been very good at being a wife yet, so I'm not really ready to take on something else until I've had some success at that."

The tiny flare in Gabe's dark eyes could have meant anything but when it continued to burn over her face, Lainey knew he was not only satisfied by what she'd said, but that he was also satisfied that she'd just given him a clear signal of her intent to stay and live up to her vows.

"Call Blake before you call Chicago."

His low voice was soft, but there was no mistaking the earthy undertone. The way he said it emphasized his desire for the sexual side of marriage and she couldn't help the feminine edginess she felt.

"You need to know that it takes a month on the pill before it's completely reliable."

"I've heard. I'll get something for the gap when we go to San Antonio."

There was no way to mistake his plan to avoid a thirty-day wait. The heat that had crept into her face began to spread lower.

"But right now, finish your breakfast while it's still hot, Mrs. Patton," he growled. "Maybe give this discussion a few minutes to cool off."

It was something of an echo of her earlier warning about his steak and eggs going cold, and Lainey smiled and looked down to go back to her food. She didn't mind at all that their conversation lapsed back into silence for the rest of the meal.

They'd gone riding and come back to the house about the time her lawyer would have arrived at his office. Lainey made that call then made a second one to see if Dr. Blake had an opening in his schedule soon. To her surprise, a cancellation for the next day had just been made and she took it.

When they'd gone to Talbot Ranch, Lainey spent a long time in the big house, wandering through, remembering. Most of the furniture sat in the silent house under sheets, and Lainey was struck by the sadness of that. If Gabe stayed married to her, she'd never live here again, and yet it didn't seem right for the fine old house to remain unoccupied.

The trip to San Antonio took the longest, partly because it was over a four-hour round trip, partly because Gabe insisted on seeing her try on more dresses and outfits than she'd planned to. He seemed to genuinely enjoy seeing her model the clothes, and before she knew it, he'd bought several things he'd liked along with the few things she'd picked out.

They'd gotten into a whispered argument when she'd insisted on paying for her own things, but he was iron-willed on the subject. The fact that he easily charmed the salesclerks into ignoring her checks and credit cards in favor of his gave him several decisive wins.

As a result, he made more than one trip to the car to stow their purchases in the trunk, and while he was gone on the second one, Lainey slipped into a jewelers farther down the mall and looked through a selection of men's jewelry to find a gift.

Though she already knew Gabe wasn't big on men's jewelry, she selected a beautiful turquoise string tie because she knew he favored those. After she paid, she tucked the box into her handbag then slipped into a store a couple doors down to shop for work jeans and cotton shirts. She managed to buy enough in her sizes before Gabe found her and could insist on using his credit card.

"There's one of those lady's stores down the way," he told her. Lainey knew instantly the one he meant was a lingerie shop, and she suddenly got the impression this might be the highlight of the day for Gabe.

He'd told her they'd buy her something with lace and ribbons when they went to San Antonio, so she shouldn't have thought he'd forget. Though she felt self-conscious about the kind of sleepwear he might have in mind, he'd been so pleasant with her that day that she was leery of doing anything that might spoil the growing companionship between them.

To her surprise, Gabe walked into the lingerie shop with her, as unconcerned and at ease about being in such a feminine place as he would have been in a cow lot. And the contrast of his earthy masculinity and rugged looks against a backdrop of sexy lace and satiny intimate apparel made it all look even more delicate and fragilely feminine.

The few other women in the store grinned at him from over the racks, and blushed when he noticed and gave a respectful nod. It was some sort of variation on the bull in the china shop, only there was no damage and the bull was completely tame.

In other shops, Gabe had pulled an outfit or two off the racks to show her. In this shop, he wedged his big fingers in his front jeans pockets, and somehow she read his preferences from the interest he seemed to show in one thing or another.

To Lainey's relief, there were a few things in the shop that were more diaphanous than revealing, and though she could tell Gabe might prefer some of the bolder ones, he didn't object to the handful she picked to take into a changing room along with some of the ones he'd seemed to like.

When she was finished, she came out in the clothes she'd worn in, and the things she'd tried on draped over her arm.

"Everything fit?"

Lainey nodded, and the clerk who'd been hovering nearby took the white floor-length gown and matching wrap Lainey had chosen. Another clerk came over to return the other things to the racks.

"Add that little blue thing," Gabe said to the clerk, unconcerned that someone nearby might hear. "And the pink—no, the pearly pink," he said, aiming a finger toward the one he meant. "Wrap 'em up with everything else."

Both clerks beamed at him as they sorted and separated out the things he'd indicated, and Lainey felt edgy. Because she didn't want to embarrass Gabe, she caught his hand to get his attention when one clerk turned away toward the register and the other hurried back to the racks.

"Oh, Gabe, this is very generous," she whispered urgently, "but I don't need all of them."

"I do."

Her protest hadn't dimmed his obvious pleasure, in fact, his dark eyes were dancing with something a lot like masculine anticipation, though his expression was solemn.

"I work all day with rough, dusty animals, Mrs. Patton. It'll be damned nice to look at something fine and silky on my wife."

Lainey couldn't help the blush that surged into her cheeks as her gaze darted around them to make sure Gabe hadn't been overheard. Suddenly she remembered how little distance there'd been between them that day, and how hugely relieved she'd been. If this shopping trip had somehow put them on more comfortable footing with each other, then she needed to take Gabe's apparent preference for buying those sexy things gracefully. She'd try not to think about how soon he expected her to start wearing them.

"Thank you," she said. "You didn't need to buy anything for me today, but it was sweet of you."

"Sweet."

Gabe said the word as if it was something suspicious. Lainey couldn't help a giggle as his expression went playfully grim, as if using the word "sweet" to describe him was somehow an insult to his rugged machismo.

"Yes," she said, enjoying this, "sweet."

"Sweet." He growled the word that time. "I don't reckon I'd repeat that to any of the men."

But Lainey could tell by the lighthearted glimmer in his dark eyes that he was not only amused, but that being called "sweet" had taken him pleasantly by surprise. There was so much that Gabe's tough exterior concealed, and she suddenly got a fresh sense of the rich treasures he'd hidden away.

That was the moment Lainey realized she'd never stopped loving Gabriel Patton. Suddenly, all her feelings for him came rushing back like a towering sea wave crashing onto a dry, empty beach. The difference this time was that what she felt for him had matured from the adolescent feelings she had for him years ago, and that staggered her.

Lainey walked with him to the service counter in a kind of daze, then looked on as he charmed the clerk who'd placed two extra boxes Lainey hadn't known about into the shopping bag with everything else.

As she watched Gabe, her emotions grew overwhelming as she more fully registered the pleasure he'd seemed to take in watching her model things for him that day, and sensed his pride and satisfaction in spending a small fortune on her.

It was almost as if there was some well of generosity in his soul that had been dammed up all his life, first by poverty then by lack of opportunity. There was no way to mistake the fact that it was now bursting free. As if he'd waited years to do something as common and husbandly as shop with a wife; as if that dam of generosity had burst for the simple reason that he finally had both the money and someone all his own to lavish it on.

Lainey couldn't help but think again about all the packages he'd sent her through the mail, and that because of the dates they'd arrived, they'd clearly been birthday, anniversary or Christmas gifts. Suddenly she could picture the pleasure he must have felt as he'd chosen each one and the hope he must have had as he'd dropped them off at the post office. She didn't spare herself the picture of the grimness, and maybe even hurt, that must have come over him when every one of them had been delivered back to him.

The worst remorse Lainey had felt so far engulfed her in that store, and she almost burst into tears right there. Somehow she managed to keep her composure while Gabe finished the transaction, but the utter misery she felt was the most excruciating of her life.

Today—and particularly these last few minutes when Gabe had shown her a bit more of his gentle sense of humor—were like little golden drops of honey falling lightly into a bucket filled close to the brim by years of hard feelings and anger. The mental picture was an accurate depiction of the dismal reality between them, and the self-loathing Lainey felt was another crushing weight on her heart.

Was it possible to somehow increase those little

golden drops? Was it possible to either wash out the bitterness in that pail or to at least sweeten the acid tang of all that her selfishness and cruelty had put there?

As Gabe picked up the shopping bag and they walked into the mall, Lainey eased her arm around his lean waist in a desperate craving to somehow make it up to him. When Gabe instantly wrapped his arm around her and pulled her snugly against his side, she felt his delight with the simple gesture, and her eyes begin to sting.

When they got to Gabe's car, they stowed the last of the bags in the trunk. Gabe walked her to the passenger side, then came around the front of the car to get in and start the engine. As if he'd sensed her melancholy, Gabe wrapped his strong fingers gently around hers and they rode in silence all the way back to Patton Ranch.

CHAPTER EIGHT

LAINEY managed to make it all the way home before she'd had to shut herself in the bathroom for a good cry in the shower. When she'd come out dressed in jeans and a T-shirt, recovered and with a fresh application of makeup, she joined Gabe in the den. He'd already showered and changed elsewhere and she noted that he wore black slacks, black dress boots and another pristine white shirt with long sleeves that he'd folded back to reveal his thickly corded tanned wrists.

He'd dressed a little more formally tonight, and Lainey was alert to that. She realized he might like to see her in one of the sundresses he'd bought her, so she slipped back to their bedroom to change into the blue one with white seersucker stripes.

Supper was served at the end of the back patio just outside the master bedroom. The round, cloth-draped wooden table Elisa had set with good china had been placed in the shady path of a nearby tree trunk that blocked the bright angle of the evening sun.

The candelabra in the center of the table hadn't been lit yet, so Gabe struck a match and quickly remedied that. All of this had to be deliberate, and Lainey was certain that it was Gabe's idea rather than Elisa's. The wine flutes on the table and the bottle of wine Gabe had just opened and poured added to the romantic presence of the candelabra, the china, and the warm outdoor setting.

It was a huge relief to have gone so far past the conflict between them, to actually feel this level of companionship and ease. Just last night things had been grim and confrontational, so today had been something akin to a miracle. Lainey had already vowed to never allow things between them to go back to the way they'd been before today, and it looked like Gabe might have decided to do the same.

Lainey couldn't help worrying about what would happen now. Not that she was as edgy about the notion of physical intimacy, but because she wanted their marriage to be based on something far more than sex and having children. Today had been a wonderful start toward that goal, and yet she was constantly reminded of the fact that she wasn't worthy to receive any of the deeper things she wanted their marriage to have, particularly Gabe's love.

That feeling of unworthiness had increased with every generous and well-meaning thing Gabe had done that day. He was still making all the sacrifices, and she was still the unquestioned beneficiary. She'd deserved none of it, not a single thing, including all that he'd done to save Talbot.

Her craving to find some way to either match or outdo his sacrifices and his generosity felt as daunting and doomed to fail as it was strong. What on earth could she give or do that was worthy of him? And his prodigious five-year head start only emphasized the notion that she couldn't possibly catch up.

"We've got time for a toast before Elisa brings the food," he said, then picked up his wine flute. The fragile piece rested easily in his strong fingers.

Lainey reached for her wine flute, then lifted it toward his. "What are we toasting?"

"You pick."

He'd gently put her on the spot, and the fact that she didn't dare offer a toast to what she truly wanted deepened her feeling of melancholy.

"H-how about...to our future?"

"Is there one?"

The low question was another painful little nick. Her voice was nearly a whisper as she said, "For as long as you say, Gabe."

He stared at her those breathless moments, poised to touch his wine flute to hers, but not making a move. "Then say it like that."

Lainey lifted her glass higher and said, "To our future...together."

Gabe touched his glass to hers and they both had

a quiet sip. He set his down and leaned one forearm on the table as he looked over at her. Self-conscious because of the intensity in his dark eyes, Lainey carefully set her flute down then toyed nervously with the stem.

"You look beautiful tonight," he drawled. "Blue suits you. Makes your eyes look a foot deep."

Gabe's compliment was blunt and simple, but it warmed her. "Thank you."

Elisa brought their steaks then, and they started on the meal. Talk was infrequent, but not uncomfortable. Mostly they talked about plans for the next couple of days, and discussed whether or not to go early to the McClain barbecue.

Afterward, they went for a long, leisurely walk in the warm evening before they eventually came back to the patio to sit on the big double swing and watch the sunset. The sky started to darken then and the stars began to wink to life in the huge expanse of blackness overhead. The lights from the headquarters and from inside the big house shown brightly enough on the patio to provide low light.

Lainey looked over at Gabe's relaxed profile, still fixated on the need to make a fuller apology to him. In spite of today and this evening, the past dragged after them everywhere, and the sadness and regret she felt about it dogged her every thought and weighted her heart. She found the courage to make a small start.

"Would I spoil all this if I..."

Lainey let her voice thin to silence. Perhaps her motives weren't right. Was it selfish to keep bringing up the subject? Gabe deserved to hear a full apology, but perhaps she was as motivated by the pain of holding it inside as she was by the sense of obligation she felt to make it. And what might make it particularly selfish was that bringing the subject up again had the potential to spoil the fine day and wonderful evening he'd arranged for the two of them.

"If you what?"

Now she saw his profile grow slightly harder, as if he was starting to withdraw from her.

"Please don't do that—don't close yourself off." Lainey touched his forearm urgently. "Please. Just forget I said anything."

"It's been eating you up all afternoon, so you might as well say it," he said as he looked at her. His eyes went somber. "Then I'll say what I'm goin' to, and we'll be done with it."

Lainey felt a shiver go through her. He had to know she was about to try again to apologize, but she couldn't tell if that last part of what he'd said was a warning or not.

She thought again of all those packages she'd sent

back, and because of her new insights into him that day, she couldn't help that her heart broke a little more. Now that he was allowing her to do it, what apology could she possibly offer that could take the sting out of all those rejected gifts and letters, along with every other rotten thing she'd done to him?

As many times as she'd rehearsed it in her mind, now that the time had come, her brain suddenly wouldn't give her anything more eloquent than a stumbling start.

"I'm—I've wanted to tell you so long, I…thought of lots of words, but…" Lainey's fingers tightened on his arm before she could make them relax, frustrated as she struggled for the power of speech. Her hand was shaking so she lifted it from Gabe's arm to grip it with her other hand in her lap.

It was even harder to keep her gaze fastened to his. If Gabe could somehow judge her honesty by something he might see in her eyes, she wanted him to have a full opportunity to do so.

"You didn't deserve a second of the hatefulness or trouble I caused you," she said softly. "I'm so sorry about that, about everything. Deeply and profoundly sorry. I'd like to make it like it never happened, but I know that's not possible." Her voice broke on the word. "Maybe I can still make it up to you somehow, some way. And maybe, if I can do that much, what I did before might fade. In your memory, I mean. In time. But whether it does or it never can, I'm still profoundly sorry. If I could do it over…''

He'd let her get out the bungled words until her own emotion and frustration squeezed them off, but even though he'd let her ramble on, all of it sounded paltry. Sick about that, she hastily added, ''It all must sound lame to you now, but m-maybe over time—if you still want me to stay—you'll see that I genuinely mean it.''

Lainey managed to get in a shaky breath. Shaky because it was so hard to hold back the flood of tears that were suddenly crowding up from her heart, but also shaky because his face had gone stony and his gaze was now turbulent.

Her nose began to sting so sharply that her gaze shied miserably from his. The last thing she wanted to do was cry in front of him, though she couldn't help that he could probably tell she was about to. She didn't think he'd scorn her tears, but she didn't want him to think she was trying to manipulate him into going easy on her.

''I accept.''

The gruff words almost undid her effort to hold back. She couldn't quite manage to look at him yet, but she slipped up a hand and curled her fingers into a fist that she pressed brutally against her lips to distract her from the prickle of tears.

When she could, she dropped her hand and looked at him. Gabe's face had blurred a little in the dim light, and she got out a strangled, "You're...sure?"

"We'll start even from here."

Lainey tried not to read any more into that than he might have meant.

"Start even?" She held her breath, hardly daring to believe this.

"Our marriage won't have much chance if we don't. The slate's clean, but I need to know something."

Lainey went a little tense again. "What's that?"

Gabe's expression seemed to go a bit tougher, and his voice was gravelly with it.

"Are you plannin' to leave anyway after the five years are up and things are settled with Talbot? Or will you stay with me?"

It hurt to hear him ask that. He'd just accepted her apology and given her a clean slate. To know he still expected she might leave him anyway was another little heartbreak. When she could speak, her words were thick with emotion.

"I won't leave unless you want me to," she whispered unsteadily.

A flare shot through his dark eyes, and she felt the glittering heat of it. He lifted his arm to drape it over her shoulders and pull her tightly against his side. Lainey put her hand on his chest.

"And thank you. I don't deserve another chance, but I want it. Very much." She quickly dashed the dampness from her eyes and tried to smile at him as she brushed her tear-damp fingers on the lap of her sundress. "I didn't spoil this beautiful night, did I?"

"Only if you don't kiss me."

The smoky timbre of his voice was seductive, and Lainey lifted her hand to his lean cheek and coaxed him down to her lips. This kiss was tender like the one that first night, but it was now heartfelt for her, though it still carried the lingering sadness of years on it.

Gabe didn't allow that for long before he pulled her onto his lap and boldly invaded her soft lips. He still tasted of wine, and his kiss had much the same effect on her. By the time he finally ended it, Lainey ached so desperately for more that it was all she could do to keep from taking it.

As if he, too, didn't want to stop, he nuzzled her hair and pressed a kiss there.

"I've got something for you," he murmured as he tightened his arms.

"You've given me several things today, Gabe," she whispered gently, then pulled back a bit to look at him, "but I got something for you today, too. Would you mind if I gave it to you first?"

Gabe tipped his head back slightly to curiously study her flushed face. "When was that?"

"During one of your trips to the car. May I?"

He grinned a little at the formality. "You may."

Lainey slid off his lap and rushed from the patio into their bedroom to the drawer where she'd hidden his gift. She'd asked Elisa for some paper and ribbon before supper, then secretly wrapped it while Gabe was checking messages in the den.

The tissue-wrapped jeweler's box with the dark blue curling ribbon wasn't very big, but after what she'd glimpsed in him today, the surprise of it might please him more than the gift itself. Lainey hurried back out to find Gabe still sitting on the swing. Though she saw no evidence of it, he must already have brought out whatever it was that he'd planned to give her. Lainey sat down next to him on the big swing and handed him the box.

He took it solemnly, then slowly tugged off the ribbon and hung the looped part that had circled the box on his little finger. It was interesting to watch him actually unwrap the box instead of simply ripping off the tissue. The sight of his big hands working so competently with the fragile paper, sent heat tingling through her as she suddenly pictured what it might be like if he touched her with that same gentle care. And then he opened the box.

Lainey was watching his face intently as he

smiled and took out the string tie. "Don't believe I've seen turquoise this fine," he said gruffly as he held it up in a stronger shaft of light. "Thanks very much, *my darling wife.*" Now he looked at her and held it up. "Will you do the honors?"

She took it from him and slid the turquoise piece down to widen the braided loop. Then she lifted it to slip the loop over his head and lower it to his neck. Lainey rolled it beneath his collar before she smoothed the white fabric down all around and buttoned his shirt the rest of the way. When she slid the ornament to the top and gently adjusted it, Gabe caught her fingers.

Lainey watched as he closed his hands over hers so that her fingers curled around his big thumbs. The sight and sensation of his warm, hard lips pressing against the backs of her fingers made her insides melt into a quivering heat that made her whole body begin to tremble. When he began to gently nibble her fingers, she felt a series of erotic quakes go through the most feminine part of her.

Too soon he stopped and released one of her hands to reach into his shirt pocket. Lainey was still staring dazedly into his dark eyes, so she didn't see what he'd taken out. When his gaze grew solemn, she felt a flutter of worry.

"Since you're stayin', I'd like you to wear these."

Gabe held up the gorgeous wedding and engagement rings she'd left lying beside her signature the day they'd married at the courthouse, and Lainey felt a fresh rush of tears.

The large stone on the engagement ring and the ones on the wedding band sparkled like a tiny galaxy, even in the dim light. Gabe had spent a fortune to give them to her, and she'd callously taken them off and walked away, unmoved by both the gesture and the cost.

Shamed and humbled and completely aware of how unworthy she was and how patient he'd been with her even back then, Lainey couldn't stop the flood of tears that popped onto her lashes then dropped in miserable streaks down her face.

"Oh, Gabe, I hate myself." The words had come out on a desperate little gust of agony.

She jumped a little when he growled out a harsh, "That's enough," that made her gaze shift up to the stern glint in his.

Gabe tenderly singled out her ring finger and slid on the rings, then straightened them before he gripped both her hands in his.

"We put everything behind us a few minutes ago, including that day at the courthouse. If you meant what you said, we go on from here." His grip tightened on her hands and he gave them a slight shake. "Got it?"

Lainey gave him a trembling smile that she couldn't quite hold. "Yes, I've got it. Thank you."

The solemn look in his eyes hinted at compassion for her tears and the reasons for them, and that made it all the harder to make them stop.

Lainey pulled her hands from his and put her arms around his neck to tightly hug him. Her body still jerked with silent sobs, and it was soon apparent that she couldn't regain enough control of herself to stop crying.

"I'm sorry," she whispered, then found herself suddenly swept up in his arms as he turned to carry her to their room. Lainey snuggled closer, her throat and chin on his shoulder as she madly wiped the wetness from her face before he could get her into the house and into the light and see them.

Once inside, he set her on her feet to pull the drapes. Lainey escaped to the bathroom to wash her face and make herself more presentable. When she stepped out, Gabe was in the big closet, prying his boots off on the bootjack.

He smiled at her when she walked to the open door, and it was truly as if he'd set aside the past. "You gonna wear that pretty white thing you got today?"

Lainey laced her fingers together in front of her. "Would you rather I wear one you chose?"

Gabe shook his head. "It's best not to start something tonight. I might be able to handle the white thing, but not the others.''

The bluntness of that sent heat to her face that only intensified as he went on.

"And just so you'll know, I want a lover in my bed. When the time comes between us, and it will soon, I don't want it to be about makin' up for anything but lost time.''

The rough charm of that, as well as the sudden erotic pictures it put in her mind, made her give a small smile. Gabe smiled, too, and her heart was jolted by a surge of love.

"You might get busy on showing more of those smiles when you get time, Mrs. Patton. They're awful damned pretty.''

"So are yours, Mr. Patton,'' she said back, genuinely meaning that.

His smile dropped abruptly from his face, but his gaze took on a dark sparkle. "Now sweet I'll put up with in private, but pretty...'' He gave his head a decisive shake. "No self-respecting man will tolerate being called pretty.''

Lainey couldn't help the giggle. "All right, how about handsome? Or maybe 'awful damned' handsome?''

His dark brows went up skeptically. "For a rough-lookin' ol' boy like me?''

"Especially for you. You have no idea what it

looks like when you smile, or how it makes me...feel.''

Gabe had taken off his string tie and started unbuttoning his shirt when they'd started this, but his fingers stopped at the button just above the waistband of his slacks.

''Well now,'' he said, his voice so low and gravelly that it was almost a rasp. ''How *does* it make you feel, Mrs. Patton?''

The sudden hush in the big closet was heavy and subtly sensual. Lainey felt the steady thickening of the air and dared to tell him.

''It makes me...feel good. It changes the room somehow, and I have a hard time looking away. And there's an ache after that makes me watch for it to happen again.'' She took a shallow breath. ''I don't think I can explain it any better than that.''

The silence and the heavy sensuality had intensified until the air was charged with it. Gabe's face went somber.

''If you explain any better, you won't need to put on that white thing.''

Gabe's masculinity seemed to reach for her and wrap around her like a giant fist. A wave of excitement and feminine fear surged through her, and her knees went weak. ''Should I...step into the other room?''

It was an idiotic question to ask, but from the look in Gabe's eyes, it was exactly the right one.

"Go on. A man can only tolerate so much before his good intentions go down the drain."

Lainey quickly turned to step out of the closet. She got her things from a drawer, and slipped into the bathroom to remove her makeup and dress for bed.

When she came out, Gabe was already there, his back propped against the headboard, and the covers settled waist high. His dark eyes burned over her as she crossed to the bed.

She'd left off the wrap and only wore the nightgown that covered her from just above mid-chest to feet. All that held up the layers of silk were the spaghetti straps. Lainey had already checked in the bathroom mirror, so she knew the nightgown didn't look quite as opaque as it had in the shop.

But she regretted leaving off the wrap the moment she suspected the gossamer layers were shifting as she walked, causing them to thin and thicken, giving glimpses then taking them away.

When she reached her side of the bed and climbed in, she quickly covered herself. Gabe snapped off the light almost right away, and slid down to lie beside her.

His low voice had softened. "You looked like a virgin sacrifice walking to a pagan altar."

Lainey glanced his way in the darkness. She hoped that hadn't offended him. "I didn't realize."

"Thought I'd mention that the first time between us—or any time—wouldn't necessarily be in a bed."

Lainey heard the hint of humor in the blunt remark, but didn't comment because she sensed there was more.

"Having a wife gives any private place…potential."

Now she spoke up. "How is it different with wives than with girlfriends?"

"More opportunities to wind up together in more places."

Her soft, "Oh," sounded impossibly virginal.

"I didn't say that to make you wonder if I'm oversexed. Just that I mean it about waiting. Not long, but not tonight."

Lainey smiled in the darkness and inched her hand over to push her fingers into his hand. Gabe turned toward her and put his arm around her. It surprised her when he didn't kiss her, but she could feel the hum of tension in his big body and understood why.

The heavenly feel of lying beside him with his arm resting heavily over her was so exciting that she dared to put her hand and forearm on the arm he'd draped across her. His wordless growl made her smile again.

She laid in the dark thinking about the things he'd said. Simple things, but so welcome that she was certain now that staying with Gabe was not only the best thing she could have done, but the one thing she'd never regret.

CHAPTER NINE

THAT next day, Gabe drove her to the doctor's appointment. Every eye was on them from the moment they walked in the door until Lainey confirmed her arrival. As she and Gabe turned to find seats, four patients said hello to Gabe then to her before they pointedly glanced at her left hand to see the rings. By the time they'd sat down, every adult in the room including the two clerks behind the arrival desk, who were still whispering to each other, had given them both a close perusal.

Gabe seemed immune to the frequent glances, but Lainey felt each one, particularly when she noticed they were focused more frequently on her than on him. It was about that time that Gabe lifted his arm and let it rest casually on the chair back behind her.

Lainey glanced toward him and saw that instead of ignoring the steady stares of the patients around them, he was returning each one. The grim glitter in his dark eyes made her risk a look to see who that grimness might be directed at. The moment she did, she saw that one by one, several sets of gazes had suddenly found something else to stare at.

Though she'd felt the censure of everyone in the

room and from the clerks behind the arrival counter, it was Gabe she felt badly for. Had people stared at him like this for years, whispering just out of earshot? Small towns could be like that. For the most part it was harmless, but Lainey couldn't help but think again of the repeated nicks to Gabe's pride.

Though no one would be able to miss it when a man like Gabriel Patton walked in, she was certain he wouldn't appreciate attracting attention for anything more than his good character and hard-won accomplishments. She'd heard enough about how he'd grown up to know that his family had frequently been the target of gossip, and that the gossip had also included him.

Gabe had overcome his difficult upbringing and worked his way up in the esteem of others while he'd worked toward his financial successes. To know after all he'd done to achieve respect that his witchy wife had again made him a target of more gossip made Lainey feel sick. Even worse, it occurred to her then that it might even be possible that a few people had considered Gabe some kind of villain who'd driven his wife away.

Lainey sat tensely, steeped in the consequences of what she'd done. Eventually she reached for Gabe's hand. He eased it over to meet hers and she warmly gripped it. She felt him absently brush his thumb over the diamonds on her rings, idly lining the engagement ring up with the wedding band then rotating one or the other so he could realign them again.

It was an absentminded task of boredom, so Lainey glanced at the abandoned news magazine on the chair next to hers. She was just about to offer it to him when a nurse stepped into the waiting room to call her name. Gabe released her hand, so she picked up the magazine and passed it to him as she got up.

Because more people were beginning to walk in from the parking lot, Lainey felt guilty for leaving Gabe alone to face the scrutiny of several more sets of curious eyes.

It was marginally less uncomfortable to go to the pharmacy to fill her prescription. At least here they could wander the aisles of the big drugstore and avoid being noticed. If someone did notice, and some had, they could cut it short by moving to another aisle. In spite of that, Lainey didn't feel so much as a quiver of relief until they were finally in Gabe's big pickup on their way to the highway and home.

She'd been about to apologize to him for the attention that day, when he spoke as if he'd known what she was thinking.

"Once they get used to seein' us together, the Dairy Queen'll get a new flavor of ice cream or some cattleman'll get twins off one of his cows, and we'll be yesterday's news.''

Lainey exhaled a nervous breath that ended on a grateful laugh. She reached over to grip his hand.

Gabe glanced her way. ''So get that sick look out of your eyes, Mrs. Patton. Folks will soon come around.'' He faced forward to watch the road as he went on.

''Not often a hard marriage straightens out, and most folks like to see that.'' He paused to negotiate a turn. ''Once they get done talkin' it to death one way, they'll talk it up the other way. Sayin', 'Ain't Lainey and her man good for each other? Salt of the earth, the both of 'em.''' His exaggerated drawl coaxed a smile out of her.

Lainey put her other hand fondly over the back of his. ''I hope so.''

He growled out a decisive, ''I *know* so,'' as his big hand squeezed hers. ''Since I can tell you're already worried about Mac's barbeque, you might as well stop. It won't hurt folks at all to see that I'm proud of my wife.''

Oh, God.

''Proud? Oh, Gabe…''

They'd stopped at the last stop light in town, so Gabe glanced at her again, his expression deadly serious.

''Takes a lot to face up to things, then work to

make them come right. Takes even more to hold
your head up and not let anyone run you off. You'll
go with me Saturday, and you'll let 'em see what
you're about now.''

Gabe glanced ahead of them just in time to see
the light change, so he started the pickup forward.

Lainey's impulse was to tell him she doubted it
would be as easy as he'd made it sound. Instead she
tried a different tack.

''I haven't done all that much work, Gabe. And
certainly very little to make anything right between
us.''

Gabe's profile went stern. ''You came back to
face up to things, you're going down the road with
me in this pickup, and you mean to stay. I've got
faith in the rest,'' he said then glanced over at her
to add, ''I've got faith in you.''

The sincerity she read in his solemn gaze caused
a bittersweet ache, and Lainey couldn't help the
sting of tears. Was she a good enough person to live
up to his lofty expectations of her?

Particularly when she could see that his expectations told her more about the disappointed yearning
in him than they did about his good faith and level
of optimism. And, oh, God please, she didn't want
give him even a whisper of disappointment.

If she wasn't noble enough now to deserve him,

she'd find a way to be. The craving to live up to his
expectations was a powerful motivator.

"What good thing did I ever do to get a husband
like you?"

Gabe's dark brows climbed high and he glanced
over to grin at her. "Watch yourself. Talk like that'll
go straight to my head."

She smiled. "So be it."

Gabe squeezed her hand again and went back to
watching the road. Lainey stared at his smiling profile, and couldn't help that her heart was bursting
with love.

Just after they finished lunch, Gabe went to the den
while Lainey went to their room to change out of
her dress into jeans and a chambray shirt. She'd
barely stepped out of the bedroom into the hall when
she saw Elisa hurry into the den. Thinking nothing
of it, Lainey continued on until she overheard
Elisa's conversation with Gabe and stopped.

She was about to step out of earshot when she
realized it wasn't necessarily a private conversation,
though it was one she didn't want to disturb.

Apparently Elisa had a family emergency con-
cerning her older sister, so Gabe gave her several
days off to take care of it. Lainey was pleased that
Elisa only had time to mention her ill sister to Gabe
before he'd instantly responded and not only given

her time off for the next week—more, if she needed it—but he'd made sure she knew he'd pay her for the days off, however many there were.

Though Elisa hastily told him she'd try to find someone to replace her for the next few days, Gabe had cut her off with a gruff order to not concern herself with anything but her sister.

The natural generosity and kindness of the man made Lainey love him all the more. It amazed her now that she'd ever thought Gabe was some hardened tough guy who was too pragmatic and socially inexperienced to bother courting a woman he might want for a wife. Hadn't he proven he was more than capable and at ease with that delicate art as he'd subtly courted her yesterday and today? Because that's essentially what he'd done.

And now his kindness with Elisa and his sympathy for her family emergency showed Lainey something else. She couldn't have gotten a clearer impression that Gabe not only counted family a far higher obligation than a mere job, but that he didn't hesitate to encourage it, even to the extent of contributing to it out of his own pocket. After all, he'd not only be paying Elisa, but also someone he selected to take her place.

Because Lainey was seeing more and more that Gabe was a remarkably sympathetic and generous man, perhaps his tough exterior and sometimes terse manner were his only protection against being targeted as a soft touch.

Elisa bustled out of the den on her way to the opposite end of the house where her rooms were, too distracted to notice that Lainey was waiting a few feet down the hall in the other direction.

She started forward and walked into the den. Gabe was leaning back in his chair staring off into space as if he were thinking of something, but the moment she came in, his gaze zoomed to hers and fixed there until she'd crossed to the desk.

"I overheard your talk with Elisa." She laced her fingers together in front of her. "That was very kind of you, Gabe."

"Can you cook?"

Of course he'd ignore the compliment, so she smiled. "I cooked all the time for mother, but you're more a meat and potatoes man."

"I'm not fussy. As long as it sticks with me, I don't care. Edible's nice, too."

"It will be."

"Thanks." He spared her a faint smile. "You wanna see that overview now?"

Lainey shook her head. "I thought I might see if there's anything I can do to help Elisa, then maybe I should have a look at the kitchen and see what's in the refrigerator for supper."

"Good idea. Come back after you're done."

The words were low and there was an undertone that sent a tantalizing heat through her. Lainey saw the lazy gleam in his eyes and was reminded what he'd said last night about wives and private places. They'd never been alone in his big house since she'd arrived, and now they'd have it completely to themselves, perhaps for several days, since he'd asked her to cook.

The excitement that sparkled through her was far stronger than her natural worry about might happen.

Her soft, "I will," was somehow more than a promise to come back later.

Elisa seemed grateful for Lainey's offer, but assured her there wasn't much to do but pack a few things, which she could handle on her own. Lainey gave Elisa her best wishes for her sister, and echoed Gabe's request to let them know how things were going when she found time.

Lainey went to the kitchen, and Elisa left the house long before Lainey had finished taking stock of the refrigerator and deciding what she'd cook for supper. She located the cooking utensils she'd need, and explored the kitchen until she found where the dishes and glasses were stored.

The phone rang several times but Gabe had picked up the extension in the den. When Lainey looked in on him later, he was still on a business call. The distracted glance he sent her way was absent of even a hint of what she'd seen earlier, so she slipped out onto the patio in the fresh air.

The early afternoon was quite hot, so she only lingered outdoors a few moments before she thought of something to take care of. She glanced toward the den and saw that Gabe was still on the phone with his back to the glass, so she walked to the bedroom doors and let herself in.

Lainey crossed to the big closet to remove the new clothes she'd bought yesterday from their various bags and boxes. As she did, she put them on hangers before she inspected them for tags and clipped them off. She got to the lingerie bag but instead of opening the two extra boxes that Gabe hadn't actually given her yet, she took out the things she'd already seen and carried them into the bedroom to lay in a drawer.

For five years Gabe had refused to go to war to keep his wife. He could have gone after her and made her listen to the facts. He could have used his control over her inheritance to force her to come back to Texas; he could have sent his lawyers to inform her of the true financial state of Talbot Ranch. She wouldn't have stayed away then.

Pride rather than choice had kept him from doing those things, but it had also been anger that had kept him from letting her know about Talbot. That same anger had driven him to wait until the five years were up, then consider petitioning the courts to make a financial claim on Talbot. Worrying Lainey with that might have been a suitable piece of revenge, though he knew he'd never follow through because of his promise to John to preserve it for her.

But five years of pride and anger, made more bitter by the rigid celibacy he'd forced on himself, had suddenly changed the moment Lainey had walked down to those corrals Monday, saying she'd do anything to make it right.

He'd taken ruthless advantage of that, both prodding and shaming her into staying with him, counting on the decency he knew her father had instilled in her in a last bid to get the marriage he'd waited so long for. If she had the honor to follow through, maybe they'd both find something worth staying married for.

He'd learned the moment he'd seen her shading her eyes to fretfully look for him, that five years of smoldering anger and sexual famine hadn't managed to destroy his feelings for her or his reasons for marrying her.

Lainey had been his choice for a wife months before John Talbot had confided his worries about Sondra somehow frittering away what was left of Lainey's inheritance, and had asked for his help.

Though Gabe had believed the revised will would eventually be changed once Talbot was back in the black and Lainey parted ways with her mother, he'd never seriously believed it had a chance to go into force for many years. Because of that, the moment John had asked him what he'd want in return for protecting Lainey, Gabe hadn't hesitated to name it.

Gabe had already planned to inform John that he wanted to start seeing his daughter with marriage in mind, so his request had been both a clear signal to John of his determination to do so and a shortcut to find out if the man approved.

Not only had Lainey shown promise of the ladylike beauty she'd now become, but she'd loved the land and loved ranch life just as intensely as he had. Because she was the type who wouldn't care whether the man she married had money or not, she seemed even more suitable for a man who'd found out one too many times that he was wanted as much or more for his money than for the kind of man he was.

And Lainey's daddy had been an honorable man with far more influence over her than her harridan mother. She'd shown an impressive sense of duty to them both that had been difficult for her to balance, though she'd managed it to her father's satisfaction.

Several times Gabe had caught her blue eyes straying curiously to him and seen the bright sparkle of interest. Even after Lainey had moved to Chicago with her mother, he'd seen that same shy interest each time she'd come to visit her father. He'd wondered endlessly if her interest in him was anywhere near as strong as his interest in her.

He'd needed little more than John asking him what he wanted out of the deal before he'd bluntly asked for marriage. His response had been everything Gabe could have hoped for. After a moment of silence, John had suddenly laughed, clapped him on the back, then informed Gabe that Lainey would be home for a visit in three weeks.

"Don't wait for me to die to get a ring on her finger, son," John had said. "Get started the day she gets home."

He'd enthusiastically shaken Gabe's hand, and declared that he'd have the marriage spelled out in his will as the main condition for Lainey to inherit Talbot.

But John had died almost two weeks later and, thanks to the will, Gabe had put the ring on Lainey's finger in the courthouse a week after that, which turned out to be the day before Lainey had originally been due home.

Had she truly loved him once as she'd claimed?

Close to four days with her under his roof had sorely tried his resolve to wait for sex. Though he was sympathetic to Elisa's family emergency and regretted it had happened, suddenly all he could think about was the fact that he was alone in the house with his wife. Lying next to her in bed for the past three nights had almost finished him off, and he knew he couldn't face another night of celibacy. He might not be able to live through another hour of it.

His brain told him it was too soon, but his body roared with need.

Lainey had just collected all the empty boxes to stack the smaller ones inside the larger ones. She stowed them on the shelves above the clothes rods, then heard Gabe walk into the bedroom from the hall.

Everything in her was suddenly attuned to his arrival, though she tried to quickly finish up with the bags and the tags she'd clipped and set in a pile. Her heart beat twice for every carpet-muffled bootstep, but she didn't look his way for fear he'd see either her excitement or her sudden nervousness.

The moment Gabe stepped into the big closet, the air pulsed with his presence. His hands settled on her waist then skimmed slowly around to her belly and lingered there, fingers splayed. He pulled her back against his big body, and the scorching heat that radiated through their clothes sent the temperature in the closet shooting through the roof.

When he pressed his mouth warmly on the side of her neck, her pulse rocketed upward with the temperature. Her knees instantly went weak, and a few of the tags she'd been holding fell from her fingers like dry leaves.

Gabe reached to take them before she could lose the rest, then tossed them to one of the shelves above the clothes rod. Meanwhile his lips continued to explore her neck then her earlobe. When he lowered his hand from the shelf, he let it wander over her, tentatively at first, then more boldly. He pressed more tightly against her and his jaw settled snuggly against her cheek.

"Feels like rain in here," he murmured against her flushed skin.

Lainey felt stroke after stroke of sensation whirl through her and settle low. If she'd had more power over her body, she might have smiled. She enjoyed the way Gabe put things, blunt but not crude. But since rain broke droughts, she knew precisely what he meant to happen now, and felt the heated swirls down low rob her of will.

"I...believe it does," she said, her voice so shaky with breathlessness that her words were barely audible.

"You picked up that quick Yankee accent in Chicago," he drawled. "Bet I can slow it down."

His big hands slid higher. The moment they

reached their goal, another huge quake went through her body before his hands moved down again and he turned her toward him.

Lainey barely had time to focus on his face before he kissed her. She was aware of nothing beyond what Gabe's lips and hands did then until she was somehow lying across his bed with his big body settling against hers.

It was silent in the big room, dim from the closed drapes, but the air was so heavy with need and anticipation that every button pushed through every buttonhole, every brush of denim on denim, and the faint stutter of callused fingers skimming over cotton, sounded like tiny strokes of muted thunder.

As piece after piece of clothing was leisurely pushed or pulled away to tumble lazily off the edge of the big bed, Lainey thrilled to the heat and feel of Gabe's hard flesh and the faint abrasion of his callused hands and masculine hair against her tender skin.

There wasn't a single identifiable word between them as they kissed and explored, though Gabe's big body was taut and trembled from the effort of his restraint the whole time.

Because Lainey's control had melted away from his first touch in the closet, she was barely aware of the moment Gabe's control snapped. Or that the tender violence of it made her cry out helplessly with joy as her body soared with his to some lofty place before gravity brought them back down. Slowly, gently, they were dragged back to earth, pausing to float on an aftershock for a precious scattering of seconds before dropping downward again to land softly in each other's arms, so drowsy from the trip that they dozed heavily.

The women Gabe had been with before he'd married Lainey had been experienced. A few of those had been jaded. He'd never noticed at the time, but now he knew exactly how tawdry and incomplete sex had been back then, because he'd just discovered this past hour what it was meant to be.

His worries about being able to hold back to give Lainey time to catch up with his libido had been well-founded. A man could only restrain himself for so long, and he'd ended up rushing her more than he'd meant to.

And yet as Lainey dozed in his arms, he knew what he'd really done. The primitive need to overwhelm her and somehow mark her as his own had made it impossible to wait another second. He'd figured she'd never been intimate with a lover, so he'd gambled that giving herself to him would forge a deep bond between them. A woman raised like Lainey had been wouldn't easily indulge in casual sex and, as he'd suspected, she was still a virgin at twenty-five. Or had been.

Though Lainey had agreed to stay with him, what would happen once she truly realized he'd forgiven her and she got over her guilt? The deep insecurities he'd managed to conceal from the world had been laid bare in these past few minutes, and he felt them more sharply than he had since childhood.

Would Lainey be happy to stay here as his wife or would she come to resent him for pressuring her? Would she resent him for rushing her into sex?

And worse, had she allowed him to seduce her so soon because she felt she owed him for his years of fidelity, or had she given in so quickly because she would have done the same, even if things had been different between them these past five years?

Even Gabe knew it was too soon to hope that she'd done it out of love. If he'd had the ability to wait, would loving words have been part of their consummation? Or would waiting a few more days or weeks have given her time to decide that she'd never be able to love him?

He reckoned he was a true pig, because after years of what she'd put him through, he couldn't have stood never knowing what it had felt like to make love to her.

He'd learned enough about sex years ago to bring her quickly to the point where her body made the choice, rather than her heart. Using her innocence against her like that had been selfish, possibly cruel, but he'd needed to have at least this much with her. His body hadn't been able to wait for her to decide whether she could ever say the loving words that he was too proud to say first.

He'd loved her all along, however angry and disappointed he'd been, but he didn't truly know how she felt about him. She'd said she'd loved him once, but could she again?

Lainey stirred in his arms and gave a soft sigh. It suddenly didn't matter to his body whether this woman loved him or not, or whether she ever would. Need moved his brain from actual thought to male instinct. The moment he kissed her, her response both comforted and encouraged him.

She was completely his...at least for now.

CHAPTER TEN

THEY'D barely found time to eat that first night. From the next day until late afternoon on Saturday, they'd lived in their own private world.

Though Gabe had the relentless habit of working from dawn till dusk six days a week, with only a half day less on Sundays, he'd turned over the running of Patton and Talbot ranches to the foremen. Business calls to Patton were forwarded to the barn office, and no one came to the house but the mail carrier.

Gabe couldn't remember when he'd spent so much time indoors, but never in his life had he been so wrapped up in any woman as he'd been in his wife.

Lainey soothed something in him that he hadn't been aware needed soothing, she'd softened him. Being with her now more than rewarded his long wait for intimacy and companionship, and she'd somehow made those bitter years worth every dust-dry second.

She was a more than passable cook, and she brought him coffee and breakfast in bed. They'd eaten one lunch at the creek, but they'd had all their other meals on the patio. She'd beat him at checkers, shyly seduced him on the creek bank then later in the living room when she'd modeled one of the two camisoles he'd surprised her with, and she'd let him join her in the shower.

For a man who'd weathered a solitary life, Gabe was as overwhelmed by her attention as she seemed to be by the force of her own newly discovered passion. The years of marriage they could have from here on suddenly seemed certain, something that would surely endure until death took one of them.

Then Saturday afternoon arrived. The increasing tension Gabe noticed in Lainey, was only a bit less worrisome than the fact that she went out of her way to hide it from him. He'd already decided they wouldn't go to the barbecue much earlier than four o'clock. Two hours before the meal was soon enough, in spite of Cassie's invitation.

Though it was important for Lainey to face folks and give them the opportunity to accept her again, Gabe would have preferred to stay home or to drive down to San Antonio for a lavish dinner somewhere. If not for the barbecue, he wouldn't share her with anyone.

He'd tell her that later, when he got enough of the crowd and had gone as long as he could without making love to her. It pleased him to know that he didn't dare tell her now, because he didn't entirely trust that she could keep herself from using her newly realized feminine powers to make him forget about going.

Gabe wasn't offended by the idea that his wife might try to seduce him with that thought in mind. Ideas about how she might do it were tantalizing enough to make him consider a way to somehow invite her to try. Lainey could seduce him anytime she liked and he wasn't particular about the reason, as long as she stayed with him after she got what she wanted.

But it wouldn't be prudent to admit that. Ever. A smart man kept his mouth shut and enjoyed every second. As he thought about their last time, he decided that four o'clock might still be too early to get to the barbecue.

Lainey chose the candy pink sundress with its tiny straps, snug, sheared bodice and flaring shirt. The white sandals she'd bought to go with it gave her a casual, summery look that was attractive, but not too dressy. There'd be a wide variety of dresses and shorts and cutoffs—even swimsuits—at the barbecue, so she'd neither be the most formally dressed nor the most dressed down.

She wore her hair loose, and the only jewelry she had on besides her rings was a simple gold heart locket on a fine chain. It had a picture of her daddy in it, but there was another little compartment on the reverse side that had room for another miniature photograph. Lainey had already decided when she'd chosen to wear it that as long as Gabe seemed happy to play rather than work, she'd persuade him to go with her to a photographer next week so they could have his photo taken.

These past two days had been like a bright romantic fairy tale, and she loved Gabe so much that it was agonizing not to tell him so. But he'd not mentioned loving her. He'd said he loved *this* about her or that he loved *that,* but never once had he come close to saying, "I love *you.*" Although Lainey couldn't imagine how Gabe could demonstrate more love for her, he'd still not said the words.

So she'd taken great care not to say them herself, though they'd almost slipped out several times. She couldn't imagine ever giving herself to any man as wholly and intimately as she had to Gabe, but she was far too vulnerable to him to risk admitting the one thing that would finally place her heart at his feet.

What if he didn't love her yet? Perhaps he'd sensed her eagerness for him to declare himself but because he didn't love her, he'd stayed on guard in order to subtly rush her past those moments when she might expect it. Unless it was perhaps because of some macho notion of manliness.

They'd mentioned the words "whimsy" the other day and he'd seemed to find being called "sweet" and "pretty" or "handsome" amusing in private, but he wasn't an overtly emotional man. He'd said that actions spoke truer than words—and it didn't take instinct to know that emotionally volatile words might never be the ones he'd be comfortable using.

Even so, if he ever did say, "I love you," it would likely be profoundly emotional for him. And his confession would not only be absolutely true, but it would also be one that he'd live up to all his life. Lainey had stopped worrying that Gabe would somehow use intimacy to humiliate her. She'd misjudged him before, but she wouldn't now. He would never do that to her. She was certain of that—of *him.*

They drove over to McClain ranch and arrived just a bit more than an hour before the meal was served. The ride had been mostly silent. By the time they drove down the mile-long road from the highway, both sides of the ranch road nearer the house were almost bumper to bumper with parked vehicles, mostly pickups of every age and condition, and SUV's.

Instead of driving ahead to the wide edge of the outer lawn around the big house where many more vehicles had been parked, Gabe stopped in the drive and neatly turned the car around to back toward the black pickup that was last in line on that side.

When they got ready to leave, they'd be facing in the direction of the highway, and though it was a long walk to the house, they'd be spared the congestion that those who'd parked closer would have to deal with later.

Gabe stopped to give Lainey a moment to step out on the road before he continued backing the car into place. If he hadn't done that, her alternative would have been to get out on the edge of the grassy ditch. She walked along after the car those few feet and waited by Gabe's door for him to get out. When he did, he took her hand and squeezed it.

"Look them in the eye, and give folks a chance," he said as he leaned down to kiss her lightly.

They turned then and walked hand in hand toward the house a quarter mile away. The walk in the hot air managed to ease only a tiny bit of Lainey's dread. Before they started around the big house to the massive patio and pool in back, Gabe pulled her against his side, and Lainey took what comfort she could from the embrace.

As if she'd been watching for their arrival, Cassie called out from the other side of the pool and waved before she rushed around it to meet them.

"Oh, my," she said as Lainey eased her arm from Gabe's waist. Cassie reached for Lainey's hands. "Pink's *my* color, darlin'. How come you had to wear it and show folks how much prettier it looks on you?''

Cassie's fingers encountered Lainey's rings and her blond brows went up as she lifted Lainey's hand to inspect them.

"Lordy, Gabe, they're just beautiful. I'll bet the shine off these'd blind a person at high noon.''

Lainey couldn't help but smile and relax a bit as Cassie made over her. Cass didn't seem to care who overheard, and a quick glance around told Lainey everyone was watching. And because Cassie still had incredible social influence anywhere she went, what she was doing was tantamount to not only conferring acceptability on Lainey, but also making it clear that Lainey was a valued guest.

Lainey gripped Cassie's fingers as she quietly said, "Thanks, Cass. This means more than I can say.''

Cassie trilled out a bright laugh, as if what Lainey had said was not only funny but charming, then she whispered back, "You were a good sport way back when, Lainey, though I know it must have about killed you. You coulda made a fool of me any number of times and didn't, so I figure I owe you at least a half a dozen favors. Besides,'' she said and leaned closer, "ain't nobody understands a spoiled daddy's girl like another spoiled daddy's girl.''

Lainey laughed then, more at ease. "You're right. We can be pretty rotten, can't we?"

"Sure can," Cassie declared. "Just so we don't get into a my-daddy-spoiled-me-better-'n'-your-daddy fight, I reckon we could end up the best of friends."

"I think that's pretty certain now," Lainey said, but Cassie ignored that to give Gabe a look of mock-horror.

"This girl still talks like a Yankee, Gabe."

He chuckled and Cassie glanced briefly toward the barbecue pit to spot where Mac and several of his cronies were seated in a growing half circle of lawn chairs. She looked back at Gabe.

"Why don't you go on over and say hi to Daddy? I'll take Lainey around and bring her over in a while."

Lainey added her agreement. "Go ahead. I'll be fine."

Gabe nodded to them then strode around the big pool to the back of the massive yard. Cassie looped her arm in Lainey's and as they walked she leaned close to whisper.

"Now don't get your feelin's hurt, but the bad news is that ol' Jeanette saw you shoppin' in San Antonio the other day and found out about your trip to town. Not more than a half hour ago, she was tellin' everyone that you're the prodigal wife. That

Gabe bought you the fine robe, put the ring on your finger, and that my daddy killed the fatted calf in time to celebrate you comin' home to your poor, longsuffering husband.''

Lainey looked at Cassie, not certain whether to be appalled or not because Cassie was amused, though it was close enough to the mark to make her queasy.

"But," Cassie went on, giving her arm a squeeze, "old lady Harmon scolded her for spying on you, then passin' that around to hurt your chances with everyone. She embarrassed ol' Jeanette half to death. Most of the women seemed to agree that folks should give you a chance, 'cause you were always good to everybody, just like your daddy was.''

Lainey couldn't help the rush of emotion she felt. "Oh, Cassie, don't kid me. Please."

Cassie's gaze turned sympathetic but showed a sparkle of orneriness. "I'll kid you and lie my head off about how much better you look in pink than me, but I'm not kiddin' or lyin' about this."

She pulled her arm from Lainey's to put it companionably around her shoulders. "By the end of tonight, all they're gonna be able to talk about is how Gabe Patton and his wife danced with each other under the stars like there was nobody else at McClain's. But then they went home early, because..." She laughed and ended with, *"Because."*

The tension and the sick weight of dread Lainey had felt lifted suddenly. "Thank you, Cassie. You're very kind."

Cassie's brows went up as she dropped her arm. "Don't let that get around. Better to let folks wonder. Besides which…"

She let her voice fade as she glanced around them and urged Lainey a little closer to the edge of the patio before she went on.

"Since old lady Harmon is too far outta earshot to scold me, I can tell you that Sally got married a month ago to a man her daddy's threatening to sue, Amy Jo's pregnant with twins, and Bobbie just dumped the most scrumptious cowboy. I'm gonna volunteer to see what I can do to get him over the disappointment."

Cass nudged her with an elbow. "And I won't be sendin' him a sympathy card."

Lainey laughed, appreciating Cassie's efforts to put her at ease. Together they made the rounds, chatting here and there with the other guests. Lainey was thrilled that everyone truly did seem friendly.

Afterward they walked over to the barbecue pit where Mac had just supervised the carving of the beef. He suddenly grabbed Lainey for a bear hug as he teased her about coming with Gabe to the barbecue instead of being his date. He led Lainey and

Gabe across the lawn to start the lines past the serving tables.

When Mac had everyone's attention, he boomed out, "Welcome to the McClain barbecue, ladies and gents!"

When the cheers died down, he added an enthusiastic, "An' I'd like to present Mr. and Mrs. Gabriel Patton!"

The crowd clapped and cheered again, and there were several male hoots along with a couple of shouted bits of male advice to Gabe. Afterward, they went through the food line and Mac seated them at his table. They ate until they were stuffed.

After ice cream was served, the country band Mac had hired began to tune up next to the dance floor that had been placed just off the big patio. Gabe led Lainey over as the first number began and took her into his arms. They danced three dances. Lainey enjoyed the livelier pace of the first two, then gratefully moved deeper into Gabe's arms for the ballad that played next.

Gabe leaned down so he wouldn't be overheard. "What did I tell you?"

"It's almost too good to be true," she said, still a bit giddy with happiness.

Gabe pressed a kiss in her hair. "I'm glad you and Cassie hit it off."

Lainey smiled. "I guess we both grew up."

"Maybe so," he drawled. "I've just recently found out how good it is to make peace, so this just adds to that pleasure."

Lainey snuggled closer. "If not for you, none of it could have happened."

"I had nothing to do with you and Cassie, and I'm not sure how much I had to do with settling things between us."

Lainey shook her head. "If you'd thrown me out that day, we wouldn't be here now." She looked up at him. "Have I told you yet that you're wonderful? And the word wonderful can be a he-man term."

"Quite a compliment, darlin'."

"You're quite a man."

A lazy grin slowly curved his stern mouth. "You sure?"

"Yes." She studied the gleam in his eyes, and suddenly knew he was teasing. "Why wouldn't I be?"

"If you aren't sure, I'd give you a fresh demonstration."

"Ah," she said, smiling faintly.

"What do you say we thank Mac and Cassie for having us over and invite them for supper soon? Not too soon, though, 'cause we're pretty busy the next several evenings."

Lainey considered it. "You don't think it's too early? What will people think?"

"Folks have been watching us for the past ten minutes. They're probably takin' bets on how long we'll stay."

Lainey couldn't help the heat in her face. "Oh."

"They expect it." Gabe's arm tightened around her. "And I've shared you enough to last me a while. I'm ready to go."

"Me, too."

The band ended the number not six beats after she'd said that, so Gabe released her and took her hand to lead her off the dance floor. Mac winked broadly at Gabe as they said their thanks and good-byes, and Cassie made Lainey promise to give her a call next week.

The ride home was swift and silent. Lainey leaned back on the headrest and let the relief and pleasure she felt deepen. Eventually she turned her head and glanced over at Gabe. It was on the tip of her tongue to tell him she loved him, but worry about how he'd respond made her hold back.

When they arrived at the house, Gabe came around the car to open her door and take her hand. They were partway up the front walk before he stopped and leaned down to swing her up in his arms.

"I'm overdue to carry you over the threshold, Mrs. Patton. How 'bout we remedy that now?"

Lainey tightened her arms around his neck and kissed him. "Another good idea. Thank you."

Gabe carried her the rest of the way to the door and easily opened it without setting her down before he stepped inside. He paused only long enough to kick the big door closed behind him before he strode through the dim house toward their room.

With every step Gabe took, Lainey felt excitement zoom through her. Though she had no other sexual experiences to compare with the ones she'd had with him, Gabe was wonderfully tender with her. Just the thought of how expertly he made love to her was enough to make her feel weak at the thought of more.

Her body was already humming with anticipation, and her hands tightened on his shoulders, pressing into the steely feel of flesh and muscle beneath her fingers and palms. Gabe walked across the room then sat down on the low chest at the foot of the big bed.

He'd started kissing her before they'd got halfway across the carpet so once he had her on his lap, his big hand began to move restlessly over her bare leg. She felt the thrill of his hard, callused fingers as they smoothed higher and higher, until they stopped just above the hemline of her sundress.

Gabe drew back from the kiss. "Let me get my boots off darlin', then we'll commence with sandals and buttons and…things. Unwrap each other real slow." The words had gone lower until they were little growls.

"I'll take care of your boots, cowboy," she said, then couldn't resist kissing him again before she eased away.

She smiled as she forced herself to intercept his big hand and gently push it back to a safer level. "But I need to be able to stand up first."

"Go right ahead," he said gruffly, then moved his hand and released her.

Lainey stood then bent down to catch his ankle, but Gabe lifted his foot and leaned back so she could pull off the big boot. When she got it off, the second one came off just as easily. Lainey straightened and boldly lifted her sandaled foot to rest it on his thigh. She saw her mistake the moment his big hand closed around her ankle and he started to work slowly at the buckle.

The sensation of his hands slowly drawing out the task as he gently teased her skin made standing on one foot a bit precarious. She put her hands on his shoulders to steady herself so he could finish. When he did, she offered him her other foot.

When that sandal was removed and dropped to the floor, Gabe kept her foot on his thigh and slowly chafed her ankle and calf with his hard palms.

"That dress is a different shade of pink, but you

look a little like one of those flamingos folks put in their yards. Sure you can keep standin' there?''

Lainey giggled at that, and slid her foot off his thigh. Gabe took her hands and held them warmly as she knelt in front of him. Looking up into his rugged face, she suddenly realized afresh how sweet he was to her, and her eyes prickled with tears.

She loved him so much! It amazed her to think of all the years she'd thought she hadn't loved him. But love had been there all along, growing in secret, swelling closer and closer to the surface.

With every glimpse of tenderness and vulnerability in him, it had tried to make itself known though Lainey hadn't wanted to acknowledge it. Until that day in the mall when she'd watched him and realized it had been there all along.

From the moment they'd first made love, it had smoldered like sweet fire in her heart, blazing higher and expanding yet more until it scorched her continually. Did she dare confess it to him now?

Gabe seemed to notice she was troubled, and he gave her hands a squeeze. ''What is it, darlin'?''

When she couldn't answer right away, the solemnity that came over him gave her actual pain, and she couldn't keep silent another moment. She could trust this man with anything, especially her heart. She'd been a fool to wait. Lainey let go of his hands to urgently place her palms on his lean cheeks.

"I love you, Gabe."

Emotion made the words come out softly. The breath she managed to get in next came out on a gust of longing and hope.

"I've loved you since I was eighteen. I thought it had stopped but it hadn't, and I've wanted so desperately to tell you. It doesn't matter if you don't love me yet."

The big room went silent for several frantic heartbeats until Gabe's low voice filled it. "Who says I don't love you?"

A sparkling volley of joy showered gently over Lainey's heart, but she didn't dare breathe as she waited for the words.

"I'd been planning to tell your daddy that I wanted to see you, to marry you if you'd have me. When he asked what I wanted for protecting you, I figured that was the time to bring up the subject. He put his answer in the will."

He kissed her then, softly and expertly, the tenderness between them especially sweet before he slowly ended the kiss. As he drew back, his dark eyes melded deeply with hers.

"I love you, Mrs. Patton. It's past time to show you again."

As big and hard as Gabe's hands were, they were adept at small things and his touch was tantalizingly light. He reached behind her to slowly lower the zipper on the bodice of her sundress before he slid the narrow straps down. He left the bodice in place as his big hands lowered to grip her waist and he stared deeply into her eyes.

"Like I said, I'd like to unwrap you slow tonight, darlin'. Let you unwrap me."

Lainey moved her hands to his shirt and lowered the turquoise piece on his string tie before she began to unbutton his shirt.

They undressed each other slowly, lingeringly, but sometime after they'd finished and moved to the bed, their lovemaking grew tenderly fierce. Later, they drifted to sleep, but not until they'd had a few more kisses and whispered a few more love words.

There'd always be a few more love words, and a few more, and a few more. Enough to make up for a lifetime of silences and yearnings, and more than enough to lavish on each other and on the children who would come into their lives one by one those next years.

They joined their land along with their hearts. Patton Talbot Ranch was massive, with a proud legacy and an impressive heritage for each of their children.

Who in their time would yearn and love and marry, then pass it on.

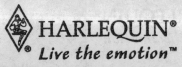

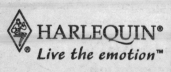

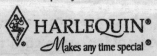

BETTY NEELS

With more than 134 novels to her name, international bestselling author **Betty Neels** has left a legacy of wonderful romances to enjoy, cherish and keep.

Be swept into a world of bliss with this wonderfully romantic, brand-new novel...

DISCOVERING DAISY
(#3746)

Daisy Gillard led a quiet life until the handsome pediatrician Dr. Jules der Huizma swept her away to Holland! Daisy thought Jules was promised to another woman.... But he was so attentive and charming she was starting to hope that she would become Jules's bride....

Don't miss this special treat brought to you by Harlequin Romance®!

Visit us at www.bettyneels.com to learn more about this beloved author.

HARLEQUIN®
Live the emotion™

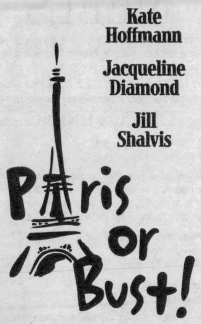

If you enjoyed what you just read,
then we've got an offer you can't resist!

Take 2 bestselling love stories FREE!

Plus get a FREE surprise gift!

Rebecca Winters

Look out for this emotional new duet by Rebecca Winters.
She's won many fans around the world with her
wonderfully compelling, sparkling stories.

Welcome to:

Twin Brides
Here come the...grooms!

Callie and Ann may look the same, but when they jet off
to Italy they meet two very different men—one's
a gorgeous prince, the other an enigmatic tycoon!

Bride Fit for a Prince—March 03 (#3739)
Rush to the Altar—April 03 (#3743)

*Don't miss this sensational duet
brought to you by Harlequin Romance®.*

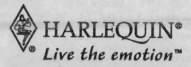

HARLEQUIN®
Live the emotion™

Visit us at www.eHarlequin.com

HRTBM03